BIRGIT VANDERBEKE

TRANSLATED FROM THE GERMAN
BY JAMIE BULLOCH

Peirene

Das
Muschel-
essen

AUTHOR

Birgit Vanderbeke, born in 1956, is one of Germany's most successful literary authors. She has written seventeen novels. *The Mussel Feast* was her first publication and won the most prestigious German-language literature award, the Ingeborg Bachmann Prize. The book was published in 1990 and has not been out of print since. It has been translated into all major European languages, including French, Spanish and Italian.

TRANSLATOR

Jamie Bulloch has worked as a professional translator from German since 2001. His works include books by Paulus Hochgatterer and Alissa Walser. Jamie has also translated *Portrait of the Mother as a Young Woman* by FC Delius (Peirene No. 3) and *Sea of Ink* by Richard Weihe (Peirene No. 9).

MEIKE ZIERVOGEL
PEIRENE PRESS

I love this monologue.
It's the first Peirene
book which made me
laugh out loud.
The author lays bare
the contradictory logic
of an inflexible mind.
This is a poignant yet
hilarious narrative
with a brilliant ending.

First published in Great Britain in 2013 by
Peirene Press Ltd
17 Cheverton Road
London N19 3BB
www.peirenepress.com

Reprinted April 2013

First published under the original title *Das Muschelessen* by
Rotbuch Verlag, Berlin, 1990
© Rotbuch Verlag, Berlin, 1990

This translation © Jamie Bulloch, 2013

ISBN 978-1-908670-08-3

Designed by Sacha Davison Lunt
Illustration by Giulia Morselli
Typeset by Tetragon, London
Printed and bound by T J International, Padstow, Cornwall

The translation of this work was supported by a grant from the Goethe-Institut, which is funded by the German Ministry of Foreign Affairs.

This project has been funded with support from the European Commission. This publication reflects the views only of the author, and the Commission cannot be held responsible for any use which may be made of the information contained therein.

Supported by

BIRGIT VANDERBEKE

TRANSLATED FROM THE GERMAN
BY JAMIE BULLOCH

Peirene

The
Mussel
Feast

It was neither a sign nor a coincidence that we were going to have mussels that evening. Yes, it was slightly unusual, and afterwards we sometimes spoke of the mussels as a sign, but they definitely weren't; we also said they were a bad omen – that's nonsense too. Nor were the mussels a coincidence. This evening of all evenings, we'd say, we decided to eat mussels. But it really wasn't like that; you couldn't call it a coincidence. After the event, of course, we tried to interpret our decision as a sign or coincidence, because what came in the wake of our abortive feast was so monumental that none of us have got over it yet. We would always have mussels to celebrate a special occasion, and this was a special occasion, although in a very different way from what we'd had in mind. Basically, what we'd had in mind when we were planning the mussel feast was pretty insignificant, certainly less important than the immensity and gravity of what actually happened. But you can't call our decision to cook mussels that evening a sign or coincidence.

Mussels were my father's favourite food, although not ours; my brother liked mussels too, whereas my mother and I never cared for them much. I don't care for them much, my mother always said as she bent over the bathtub, alternating between the small kitchen knife and the scrubbing brush, her hands bright red from cleaning mussels under the cold tap; she had to scrape, scrub, brush and rinse several times because my father hated nothing more than grains of sand crunching between his teeth. The sound drove him round the bend. I really don't care for them much, my mother said that afternoon too, blowing on her icy hands. But it was a special occasion and that's why she'd gone and bought four kilos. She thought my father would enjoy a feast of mussels when he returned home from his business trip, because he'd usually had enough of the fried and grilled lumps of meat he was served up on his trips, and so he would ask Mum to make him some decent food, something home-made at any rate; he never got anything like that in the conference hotels. He was fed up with these conference hotels; they may be comfortable, but they're not cosy, he said. My father hated going away on business trips; he preferred to stay at home with the family, so his return was always a special occasion. It was our custom to have jacket potatoes with quark and linseed oil, sometimes pea soup, too, and because my father had eaten this food as a child, he'd often request it for nostalgic reasons. He never actually asked for mussels since my parents always cooked mussels together. So for Mum to be scrubbing the mussels on her own that day, her hands bright red under the cold tap, was unusual in itself; it was quite normal, however, for her to say, I don't care for them much. It was what she always said when my parents scrubbed mussels in the bathroom together, taking it in turn to bend over the tub so that neither became too stiff. For a good hour the bathroom would resound with my father's laughter and my mother's squealing and in the past you might have heard them singing the old workers' song 'Come, Brothers, to the sun, to freedom', which they'd learned over there and were forced to sing; 'This is the final struggle' and songs like that, my mother with her soprano voice and my father in his baritone. But later, when we were in the company accommodation, they didn't sing any more. When they came out of the bathroom with bright-red hands they'd look a bit sheepish after all their larking around, and they'd continue messing about in the kitchen. Over time we found out that when they'd gone on their delayed honeymoon to my uncle's, he'd cooked them a dinner of mussels. They'd never tasted mussels before, because of course there weren't any mussels in the East, so they must have seemed rather exotic. They also thought there was something suggestive about mussels, something naughty, and they always started flirting when we were having mussels; as a result of the delayed honeymoon by the sea, flirting was routine at our house when mussels were on the menu. And remained so until that day, which we knew in advance was a special, even historic day for our family, for this business trip was to be the last step on my father's path to promotion. None of us doubted that my father would gain his promotion; for weeks we stayed as quiet as church mice on Saturdays and Sundays while he was writing his lecture and also drawing several colour transparencies by hand; we always said how beautiful these transparencies looked; so, what do you think of them, my father asked, and again we'd say how particularly beautiful they were. We already knew that my father was a brilliant and highly influential speaker; he was known for, and very proud of, his extraordinary didactic skills which he unfurled during these lectures. He also possessed a very winning and endearing manner with the public, a natural charm in addition to his expertise in one of the most difficult and controversial areas of science. This endearing manner with the public softened the rigour of his expertise, and audiences were consistently delighted by the lectures and by my father himself. That evening my mother, alternating between the small kitchen knife and scrubbing brush in her bright-red hand, was holding the mussels one by one under ice-cold water, all four kilos of them, scraping and scrubbing and rinsing several times – since my father couldn't bear the crunch of sand between his teeth – because he would be coming through the door with his promotion virtually in the bag; not officially of course, but he'd been given the nod from above. Though Mum grumbled jokingly that she didn't care for them much, and complained about her crooked spine, still we weren't allowed to help; leave it, if there's any sand in them then at least neither of you will be to blame, my mother said. But we were allowed to cut the chips; you always have chips with mussels, I don't care for them much, either, even though Mum cooks the best chips I've ever tasted. My brother, on the other hand, goes crazy for them, they're unrivalled, he always said; once he even invited all his friends who doubted and teased him about the chips to our house, and my mother made chips for them all, and my brother was terribly proud of her. Since then we'd sometimes help prepare the chips; that evening we peeled the potatoes and cut them into thin batons, increasingly feeling twitchy. Afterwards we said that this was when we started to become anxious, when we suspected something was up; of course it was only afterwards that we knew what would happen. So maybe we were simply twitchy because we were waiting; we always felt twitchy when we waited for my father, there was always a certain tension. We may well have exaggerated the tension in retrospect; perhaps we didn't suspect anything at all. My brother, for example, didn't sense anything, while Mum and I did feel anxious, but then again we're the anxious ones in the family, whereas my brother only gets anxious when it's inevitable; until then he can quite happily ignore hints or signs of foreboding. I, at any rate, can remember precisely when my mood suddenly changed: when I looked at the clock and saw that it was three minutes past six. At three minutes past six my mood shifted from an anxious anticipation to an uncomfortable, even uncanny, feeling. My mother had put the mussels in a pot beneath the kitchen clock, and as I heard the noise I looked first at the mussels and then straight at the kitchen clock. The noise was coming from the mussels, which had already been cleaned and scrubbed; they were sitting in the large, black enamel pot that we always used, because it was the only one large enough to hold four kilos. My mother had fled from the East with this pot, she told us; it was indispensable for washing nappies, and she used to wash our nappies by hand, or rather with a wooden spoon. I asked whether it wasn't impractical to flee with a massive pot like that; in my mind I had a ridiculous picture of her escaping over the barbed wire, dragging the enormous pot behind her, but Mum said, you've got completely the wrong idea about the flight, I mean we didn't just make a dash for it, we prepared well in advance. We loved listening to how she managed to move all our stuff to West Berlin, and to the story about the bananas, too. My father was almost arrested at the border, on his very first and in fact last trip to Berlin. He must have acted very awkwardly; even he admits that he's no good at such clandestine business. The only time he dared to bring anything across the border, he was too cocky, trying to take back two kilos of bananas from the West. They caught him immediately, hauled him out of the underground, interrogated him and everything, but in the end they let him go. I don't know if they really arrested people for a few bananas, seeing as half the country was trying to escape; I can't imagine that was the case, but my father says that it was resistance, political resistance. In any event he never went back and my mother brought the big enamel pot to her friend. She always took me with her when she went to Berlin; mother and child looked less suspicious and anyhow she needed to go to the Charité Hospital because I had a problem with my hip. She simply got out of the train en route and handed the things to her friend, that's what she always told us; on the way there we were wrapped up in winter clothes, on the way back we weren't wearing very much. It was risky; your father's no good at such clandestine business, my mother said when we showed surprise at the story with the bananas.

Anyway, the noise came from the pot and as I glanced over I couldn't help looking at the clock, too: it said three minutes past six. And at that moment my mood changed abruptly. I stared at the noisy pot and although I knew that the mussels were still alive, I didn't know that they made noises in the pot, because I was never around when my parents cooked mussels. Initially I wondered whether the noise was coming from somewhere else, but it was distinctly coming from the pot, and it was a distinctly strange noise, which made me feel creepy; we were already twitchy and nervous, and now there was this noise. I stared at the pot and I stopped cutting the potatoes into batons, because the noise was driving me mad, and the hair on my arms stood on end. This always happens when I get a creepy feeling, and unfortunately it shows, because the hair on my arms is black, so now my mother could see that I was spooked, although she didn't realize the cause was the noise of the mussels from the pot, as for her it wasn't a strange noise. Can't you hear anything, I asked. Listen! It's the mussels, my mother said, and I remember saying, isn't it awful, I mean I knew that they were still alive, it's just that I'd never imagined that they would make that rattling noise with their shells. I'd imagined they'd be cooked, eaten, and that was it. And my mother said, they're opening up and then the entire heap of mussels will start moving. How horrible, I thought, the entire heap of mussels will move because they're opening; of course I didn't empathize with them; I do eat them, after all, even if I don't particularly care for mussels, and it's obvious that they're alive beforehand and not alive when I eat them. I eat oysters, too, even though I know that they're still alive when I eat them, but they don't make that noise. Actually I was kind of angry at the mussels for opening instead of lying silently in a heap; I said, don't you find it obscene that they open and make that noise, obscene and indiscreet, but at the same time I probably thought it was indiscreet because we were going to kill them. I'd rather not have had to think about the fact that they were alive beforehand; when they're lying there, jet-black and closed, you don't really need to imagine that they're alive, you can pretty much regard them as objects, and then there's no problem tipping them into boiling water, but if you consider that they're alive then it's creepy. If we were to cook them now I wouldn't be able to stop thinking that we were killing them. I'm quite happy for animals to be killed for food, it's just that I don't want to be involved in the killing – other people can do that – nor do I want to have to think about it.

Although I found the mussels creepy, I went over, as I didn't want to be cowardly; and they looked revolting, lying there, some opening slowly, fairly slowly, and then the entire heap of them started to move with this rattling sound. Unbelievable, I said, how revolting these creatures are, gasping as instead of seawater they get air, which they can't breathe, and they're also being scalded in the boiling water, and then they all open, which means they're dead. The thought suddenly occurred to me that maybe it was only revolting because I knew we were killing them. Maybe it wouldn't have looked so disgusting otherwise; I remembered having seen half-open mussels on the beach without feeling anything. I even threw some of them back into the sea, not out of any real pity and not all of them – just for fun. Anyway, I didn't find them creepy or revolting like these ones here. My mother and brother cut the last few potatoes into batons, acting as if they hadn't been listening, and finally I said that if you knew someone was going to die in an hour, let's say, do you think you'd find them revolting; I'm positive you would, simply because you knew, and it would be even worse if you had to kill them yourself, like we were killing the mussels. Such thoughts plunged me into a really morbid mood, while the other two acted as if they weren't listening; it's mass murder, I said, all of them at once, at the same time, by boiling water; the mussels got me so worked up, the mussels had created a morbid atmosphere in the room. It's unbearable, I said, to which my mother replied sternly, what are you talking about, although Mum harboured plenty of fanciful ideas herself; when my father was on business trips the three of us told each other the most fanciful stories, without ever being appalled. Before my father came home, however, all these fanciful ideas vanished, especially my mother's. My father regarded flights of fancy as childish, my father stood for sober objectivity and reason, and of course my mother showed consideration for his objectivity and reason, conforming and switching to wifey mode when he came home. And when my mother said, what are you talking about, I knew at once that she'd switched to wifey mode, and the rage of disgust which I felt towards the mussels was now directed at my mother. Aren't we allowed to think any more, I said, but my mother said, is that what you call thinking, can't you think something useful rather than those sinister thoughts. In our family sinister thoughts and fantasies were regarded as squandered thoughts, especially when my father was at home, and although he wasn't there yet he might arrive at any moment. Can't we make them close again, I asked. I don't think thoughts can be squandered, because by their very nature they're the loveliest way to while away the time. Eventually I discovered that the mussels close when you put a knife into them; it triggers some sort of reflex and the mussels close rapidly again. Look, I said, taking the small kitchen knife that Mum had used for cleaning, and stabbing it into the mussels, one by one, the rattling no longer bothering me; they closed instantly. I stabbed and stabbed again. I actually encouraged all the mussels to close, and watching them close was comforting; I wasn't at all bothered when my brother said, you're crazy.

The chips had all been cut and my mother said, right, it would be good if he arrived now. Dinner was already late, we always ate at six o'clock because my father came home from the office at half past five; first he'd read the paper and drink his beer in peace while Mum prepared dinner, and at six on the dot, as I said, we ate, except when he was away on business, then the schedule went by the wayside and everything was different. There were cheese rolls and hot chocolate, we ate whenever we wanted to, sometimes standing up in the kitchen and with our hands. I don't think we ever ate with a knife and fork when my father was away. We let our hair down while you were away, Mum said when my father asked, what did you get up to without me; it's really nice to let your hair down a bit sometimes, Mum continued slightly wistfully, because she had as much fun as we did and less work, too, when we were alone with her. We seldom argued, and I liked it when we let our hair down, but my father didn't want to hear any more of it and so she switched to wifey mode. As it was now getting on for seven o'clock she'd already switched. We were all expecting him to come through the door and ask, so, what do you have to say, because his promotion was virtually in the bag, and we would have said what a clever, successful father we had, and my mother would have been pleased, too, and then we would have celebrated his success, listening to him talk about his business trip, and we would have completely forgotten our wild behaviour – only: it was seven o'clock and he hadn't come back yet. So Mum's wifey mode appeared silly and pointless; my brother even said, we're sitting here all dressed up and nowhere to go. This didn't stop my mother dashing into the bathroom and, as a precaution, combing her hair and reapplying her lipstick, which she had already put on an hour earlier; she walked around with her evening face on display, saying, he'll be here soon. My mother would often switch modes several times a day, and for each switch there was a change of face. At school she wore her serious face and was strict. She tried to replicate this face at home, but it never worked with us. We weren't afraid of her in the slightest, although her pupils were; her school face was really scary. Once my brother and I sat at the back of her class and listened in. We could have died laughing – she looked so strict, we couldn't actually believe that this woman was our mother. Respect is essential, she said; my father, too, said that respect was essential, an absolute necessity, otherwise you don't learn anything; but it never crossed our minds to show our mother respect. At home she wore her knackered, exhausted face, her household face; when she came back from school in the afternoon, she said, I'm knackered today, I don't have much energy after six hours of school. My father often said, how are you treating your mother, kindly show her some respect; in vain my father tried to instil in us the respect for our mother which she could not command from us herself. He said, can't you see how she's slaving away for you two, she grafts all day long. Of course we could see her grafting and slaving away, lugging heavy bags. When my father came home in the evening, she continued to graft and slave away, and if there wasn't any beer she'd dash out, for his cigarettes, too, and everything else my father had forgotten on his way home, she would dash out to get it in the evening. My father was a heavy smoker, and Mum often had to dash out, but he couldn't stand my mother's knackered face, and so she switched to her after-work face, which she would paint on quickly in the bathroom at half past five, before my father came home. But this after-work face only lasted for an hour and needed reapplying. Now she was walking around with her after-work face on display, saying, he'll be back soon, and I thought, I can't stand all this switching. When my father was away on business I used to have more respect for Mum; although she tried to be strict then, too, we basically got on well when there wasn't any switching. Most importantly, she couldn't spend the evenings telling my father about what we'd done wrong, so we had more respect for her. Sometimes she said, isn't this nice, children, just the three of us, probably because she found switching modes strenuous too. But when I asked, why do you bother conforming and switching to wifey mode, she replied, that's what it's like when you're married and have a job, you'll see. I'm pretty sure I won't switch to wifey mode, I said; she just laughed at me, saying, you won't find a husband anyway. She was seriously worried that nobody would ever marry me, unlikeable as I was, and unappealingly stubborn since early childhood. Luckily I never regarded my ultimate aim in life as being to switch to wifey mode at half past five every evening. I didn't like it when Mum switched; I found it embarrassing, and when we did it, too. I preferred us when my father was away on business. You see we all had to switch for my father, to become a proper family, as he called it, because he hadn't had a family, but he had developed the most detailed notions of what a proper family should be like, and he could be extremely sensitive if you undermined these notions.

But now, as it was already seven o'clock and he still hadn't arrived, my father was undermining his own notions. Mum's after-work face seemed a complete waste of time, and the mussels started making that noise in the pot again. My brother was the only one of us who was still looking forward to his mussels and chips. Mum and I had lost our appetites and were both edgy. It was the waiting. If my father had come back at six we wouldn't have noticed how silly and pointless it was for us to switch, Mum to wifey mode, we to child mode. Shortly after seven Mum said, I do hope nothing's happened; and out of pure spite I retorted, what if it has, because all of a sudden my father was a spoilsport in my eyes, or, to be more precise, a mood-wrecker. Suddenly I no longer wanted him to come home, even though an hour earlier, as I said, we all were prepared for him to walk through the door and ask, so, what do you have to say, because he'd been successful. Mum looked at me, not as horrified as I'd expected, but with her head to one side, and then

she smiled and said, well, we'll see, and she didn't
sound as if she'd find it surprising or even terrible
if he didn't come home. And gradually we stopped
thinking that he'd arrive at any moment. Only we
didn't know what to do with the mussels, which
were still rattling away quietly in the pot because
we'd thought my father would be at the door at six
on the dot, his promotion virtually in the bag, and
that would have been good reason to celebrate with
a mussel feast. My brother's mood also turned, and
although it was not yet eight o'clock we all knew
that this day was special, unexpectedly so. Only
we couldn't decide what to do. So my mother went
and cooked the mussels. We couldn't just leave them
to die, so she cooked them quickly and I thought,
who can eat mussels now; in fact none of us ate any
mussels, although my brother did eat some chips,
which Mum made while the mussels were cooking;
later the mussels sat in a huge bowl on the table and
nobody touched them. As if they'd gone off and
were poisonous, my mother said, but my brother
said, toxic, not poisonous, because we didn't say
poisonous in our family any more; for some time
now we'd been saying toxic, my mother had said
poisonous by accident. Our family used different
expressions now; for example, when we burned our
mouths on potatoes that were too hot we no longer
shouted, Christ that's hot; sometimes we still said

it by accident, because we hadn't switched modes, but my father would say, potatoes have a high heat capacity, that's the more accurate way of putting it. But when my father was away on business we burned our mouths on potatoes as before and shouted, Christ that's hot, and Mum said that the mussels looked off and poisonous, and when my brother said toxic she laughed and said they'd become truly inedible. Afterwards we wondered whether by then we already knew what was up, but of course we couldn't have known; we talked the whole time in hushed tones, as we still imagined that the door might open at any moment and he'd be standing there and catch us talking about him, and that really wouldn't be right: instead of being delighted to see him and jumping up to welcome him back home, we'd be caught red-handed talking about him, and nobody wanted that. Anyway, nobody dared to because he could be extremely sensitive and unpleasant, he couldn't bear people whispering behind other people's backs; but after I'd said, well, so what if something has happened to him – out of pure spite because my mother had already switched to wifey mode, but she hadn't reacted horrified, only saying, we'll see – after that, for it sounded as if she didn't think it so terrible either, we wondered what we would do if he didn't come back now, and soon it turned out that both my brother and I would prefer him not to come home; we no longer liked being a proper family, as he called it. In truth we didn't see ourselves as a proper family. Everything in our lives revolved around us having to behave as if we were a proper family, as my father pictured a family to be because he hadn't had one himself and so didn't know what a proper family was, although he'd developed the most detailed notions of what one was like; and while he sat in his office we played at being this, even though we'd far rather have let our hair down than be a proper family. Of course, all this came out very hesitantly; to start with I kept quiet because I thought, if he does eventually come back then Mum will blab, and my brother also thought she'd blab, and I thought my brother would blab, too, because he wants to play the loving son with my father, and my brother thought that I'd blab because I wanted to show that I was Daddy's girl. In those days, you see, we still said that I was Daddy's girl, and my brother was Mummy's boy, as my brother was very affectionate, a cuddly boy, and was forever kissing Mum. I didn't, I wouldn't have any of that; I take after my father, I thought, who was a logician, and my mother and brother were anything but logicians. And that's the reason why we, my father and I, always mocked them. And they were very wary of saying anything to me, complaining to me about my father, because they thought I'd blab about them to show everyone I was Daddy's girl. In actual fact all of us blabbed, everyone blabbed about everyone else if I think about it, and my father was burdened by the family's blabbing, even though he'd enjoy it as well, for it meant he was very important in the evenings, resolving matters in his family as he imagined happened in proper families. He'd drink beer and cognac and interrogate us in order to find out what had been going on, and we gave our statements in turn while the others waited outside. In the end he'd draw logical conclusions, fix punishments and mete them out; we were all pretty scared, to be honest, because the punishments were fixed according to logical conclusions which none of us could really understand. I pretended to understand them; it was to my advantage if they believed I was Daddy's girl and therefore logical, although in truth I couldn't really understand my father's logic and only pretended to. Neither of the other two could pretend. It was clear they belonged together because they're cuddly rather than logical, forever wanting to give each other kisses; while I belonged with my father, because I'm logical and I think, which isn't always the case with girls, but it's far better than kissing. Of course my father would have preferred our characters to be the other way around, for my brother to be the logical one, and my mother and I the ones who weren't logical, but our relationships weren't arranged in the way he thought they ought to be in a proper family. What the boy lacked was wasted on the girl, he said, but overall I wasn't as badly off as my brother, who was the younger one, too. But maybe my mother was worst off, as she had to ensure that we behaved like a proper family, surely a Herculean task given my father's notions about what constituted a proper family; they may have been incredibly precise, but were impossible to fathom as none of us understood the logic behind them. Especially not my mother, who did what she could, but, in doing what she could, she very often got it totally wrong; even though she blabbed as she ought to in a proper family, it often rebounded on her. And that evening, when she realized he wasn't coming home, she said, you can't imagine how it is, and then she said, I get really scared sometimes. Why, we asked. Although we were relieved, hearing our mother's confession felt extremely unnerving; besides, none of us could be certain that the door wouldn't open any second.

The mussels sat silently in the bowl; they were dead. And now my mother was worried that our behaviour was too insubordinate; she complained that she'd made a massive effort with our upbringing, but we knew she'd never dared contradict our father, whose promotion would definitely be in the bag now; she had massive respect for our father because he was a scientist, which was better than being an aesthete. Back then the deal was that I'd take the science route, too, because music and literature, all forms of culture in fact, were deemed hobbies, and there could be no progress in the world if scientists and engineers didn't investigate and act with rigour and resolve; whereas music, my father said, was pure excess and would never get any engine started. He said this because ever since their escape to the West my mother's violin had lain in their bedroom wardrobe, and only occasionally, when she was sad, would she sit at the piano, playing and singing Schubert songs, the whole of the *Winterreise*, back and forth, crying all the while. She sounded dreadful, even though her voice must have been beautiful at one time. We only ever heard her play the violin once, when she also cried, and we bit our lips to stop ourselves from laughing, because her playing sounded ghastly, a real cacophony; she sobbed, saying that it was not surprising her violin grated so horribly. It sat in the cold wardrobe, that was no place for a violin, and she hadn't played it for years; then we felt sorry for her. One day she took her violin out of the wardrobe – she'd occasionally take it out in secret – only to find it broken; she sat on the bed in their ice-cold bedroom, staring at the violin and sobbing, and then returned it to its green case, a proper burial: she buried the violin case in the wardrobe and came tear-stained out of the bedroom. My father hated my mother's tears and sentimentality, but sometimes he'd hug her, soothing her, come on, you've got us, haven't you, only so she'd stop; sentimentality sent shivers down his spine, the tears come too easily, he said to my mother. My father regarded himself as a man of reason, and considered abstract logic to be a thing of great beauty. Whenever my mother said, such a shame, your lovely baritone voice, a shame you never make anything of it, he would become rather dismissive and embarrassed, even though mathematics and music basically have a lot in common, my parents never talked about the similarity, unfortunately; it never occurred to them: my mother because she thought that she was an emotional person, she loved picking flowers and twigs, she'd always come back from walks with flowers and twigs, much to my father's annoyance; while my father never talked about the relationship between music and maths because he was focused on getting engines started. My mother, too, thought that engines needed to be started, but sometimes she suspected that beauty got rather short shrift; she always found logical thought dry and inconceivable, and in the evenings my father's logical conclusions gave her no pleasure. The beauty of these conclusions remained a total mystery to all of us; he was the only one in the family to sense this beauty, and that evening, when the mussels were sitting in their bowl on the table in front of us, the beauty problem appeared even more obscure, but still our mother tried to tone down our behaviour, saying that we'd been a happy family, too, reminding us that we'd always eaten mussels, and even the preparation for a mussel feast was good fun. But then she didn't sound so sure, because she didn't care too much for mussels, and I said, well, I'm never eating mussels again, for me the fun's over, and I got goose bumps again; the hair on my arms stood on end when I looked at the mussels in their bowl and thought of how they'd opened in the pan, their surrender; of course you can't call it surrender, their opening and closing is purely mechanical, and yet surrender came to mind. I loathe surrendering; I've always striven to be strong and courageous. Then, tentatively, I said something that had often struck me: why in this world does everything have to keep going on, why can't it stop; I think this going on and on should stop; and my brother added, yes, especially the torture, the torture of humans. Shhh, my mother said, as she was afraid he might hear us; he wasn't there, of course, but that was what we were like, we thought he knew everything and could see and hear everything, even though we realized how impossible this was; then again, with everyone blabbing about everyone else, he did manage to find out a lot. Mum always said that we had to stick together, and she said it that evening, too. If we all stuck together then we'd be a proper family. They'd stuck together, too, when the entire village was outraged by the marriage; my parents' marriage turned into an awful scandal, an awful village scandal, but my father didn't want an abortion, out of the question; after all, he had a sense of responsibility and morals, even when he was young he had them in spades, and so they needed to stick together while my father studied, and even more so later on in the refugee camp, because he was logical and abstract, whereas my mother was simply concrete and practical. If they hadn't stuck together it would have ended badly. Once, in the camp, my father tried to work as a builder for a day, but stopped in the afternoon. I'm not cut out for that sort of work, he said; he loathed and despised all menial work, and it was good that they stuck together. My mother earned money and did menial work, boiling the nappies in that huge pot, and cooking and shopping and children, all of which drove him nuts; my father was not cut out for such trivial jobs, and back then we would have frozen if my mother hadn't lugged sacks of coal. If I didn't have you, he said, but the refugee camp still drove him nuts, for there were no decent jobs for him; he found the endless dealings with officialdom too inane, the red tape, the bureaucracy involved in housing, food vouchers and work permits; our mother was far more adept at sorting these out. One child on her left hip, another on her right, and brazening out the queuing; she was better at howling in front of officials, too: it worked. You do it, you cry so well, my father said, it all works much better when you do it. Just please don't flake out, he said, too, when she had to repeat her teachers' exam in the West. I don't know how I'm going to cope, she said over and over again, but my father hated weaklings, these people who crack under pressure, he said, who skive off work at other people's expense; he couldn't stand illness, either. When my mother fell pregnant for the third time, in the camp, and said, I can't manage a third one, he laid into her; after all, he'd been a moral person from an early age. And then the abortion went wrong: she was laid low for a few weeks and their marriage, their sticking together, almost didn't survive. What do you look like, my father said to her every morning when she got up in her dressing gown to make the coffee and get the children ready for kindergarten; they'd agreed that life had to go on as usual. Somehow it has to go on, they said, and my father always insisted that business went on as usual and in an orderly fashion. My God, you look miserable, you're moping around with that miserable face, he said, why don't you make more of yourself, you should go to the hairdresser's sometime, he'd say; your hair is really unflattering, you're letting yourself go. My father came from a poor background and so he knew how easily one could go down in the world. That's why we always used a white tablecloth for supper; as soon as we'd left the refugee camp and moved into our own flat we unpacked the white tablecloths which my mother had brought to West Berlin, and we used a fresh one every day. Occasionally my mother would ask whether an oilcloth might not do, to save on the washing and mangling – of course we had no washing machine in the beginning – but my father was insistent: when you start going down that path, he said firmly, the place soon starts to reek of poor people. My father couldn't stand the smell of poor people and later on he was always very generous, giving huge tips when paying the bill in restaurants; he always paid the bill because the man pays the bill, and sometimes Mum asked whether it had to be such an exorbitant amount. They didn't even have enough money to last till the end of the month, and she showed him the calculations of the outstanding household bills. But he put his arm around her, pinching her hip; what wonderful miserliness, he laughed, I love your penny-pinching stinginess, and added, but if you're too stingy you look poor. Then my mother said, why should we be worried by what the waiter thinks; her thoughts were concrete and my father's abstract, he was more concerned with principles; in this way they stuck together well. But now it was past eight o'clock.

I don't know what would have happened if we'd been able to eat at six o'clock as usual. It's astonishing how people react when the routine is disturbed, a tiny delay to the normal schedule and at once everything is different – and I mean everything: the moment a random event occurs, however insignificant, people who were once stuck together fall apart, all hell breaks loose and they tear each other's heads off, still alive if possible; terrible violence and slaughter, the fiercest wars ensue because, by pure accident, not everything is normal. Broadly speaking, that's what happened. Occasionally, although not until afterwards, we said that maybe we would have stuck together like the real family we had pretended to be if the delay to our routine hadn't occurred. Maybe even if the telephone had rung earlier; but in fact the phone rang much later, by which time the delay was a few hours rather than just two, although two hours might have been enough to destroy the family; as I've said, even small delays can lead to the greatest calamities. Once, in the past, our family unity was endangered when Mum forgot the salt on holiday. We always brought hard-boiled eggs for our trip, my mother put salt into a little paper parchment bag, and if anybody wanted a hard-boiled egg in the car she'd give them the salt bag; hard-boiled eggs taste revolting without salt, they don't go down well without salt. On one occasion, however, she forgot it amidst all the packing, and there were eight eggs, two each, but no salt as a proper family should have with them on holiday; this is the end, we all thought.

We didn't watch the news that evening, either; it had gone eight o'clock and nobody thought of switching on the television. We sat at the table with an eerie sensation because things weren't normal. Had we turned on the television we'd just have been pretending; the evening had stopped being normal long before then, but it became even less normal; the abnormal situation that existed shortly after eight o'clock – with their low specific-heat capacity the mussels had long gone cold – was made even more abnormal by our failure to watch the news as usual; we intensified the abnormality in whichever way we could.

And so the mood turned sour and toxic, which is why all of sudden I said out loud what up till then I'd been quietly thinking to myself: he really knows how to spoil the mood. This abnormality, you see, had taken me right out of the celebratory mood we had forced ourselves into; only now did I realize I hadn't been in that mood spontaneously, I'd put it on like a dress because we had to stop letting our hair down in preparation for my father's return; and then my mother said, if he came now we would really spoil his mood because we're not being celebratory. Now all three of us had said it, we were no longer worried that one of us might blab to my father later; and my brother said, we always spoil his mood anyway, which was true, because my father's mood was completely spoiled whenever he heard that my brother had received another Four at school; I often lied and unfortunately he often found out that I'd lied, and that he couldn't abide. Having to get to the bottom of the truth in the evenings – even if he could see and enjoy the beauty of logical conclusions – as well as meting out punishments and restoring order in his family, spoiled my father's mood until long after the news. We said we'd ruined his whole life, and he said it too, this endless disappointment with my family is ruining my life; his family represented nothing but a disappointment to him, especially his children; but my mother, too, must have been a continual disappointment. She may have acted all jolly at half past five, but just before she'd dash into the bathroom to backcomb her hair; my mother's hair is fine and soft and, despite the perm, her hair collapses when she's exhausted and it looks sad. She wasn't particularly good at backcombing because backcombing didn't interest her; she didn't think you needed a backcombed hairdo to look beautiful, and sometimes she tried to fix her hair with hairspray, but to no avail, her hairdo collapsed regardless. She'd quickly put on some lipstick, too, and as it had to happen so quickly, when she opened the door and my father came in she'd often have lipstick on her teeth, and the sight spoiled my father's mood altogether, because the ladies in his office, his secretary for example, were pure eye-candy. One weekend he stood at the window and tears came to his eyes when he saw boys playing football outside; my father had played football, too, as a boy; in fact he played it very well, everything my father did he did very well. So he saw the boys playing, my brother was playing with them, but my brother was not very good at football; actually he just stood on the side looking awkward and clumsy, hoping that the others would forget he was there and not pass to him. Sometimes he pretended to run a bit in the wrong direction, to avoid looking as if he was rooted to the sidelines, and my father stood at the window, behind the dining-room curtain, and he saw how awkward and clumsy my brother was, and how dreadfully afraid of the ball he was, and my father even said, he's running away from the ball, and tears came to his eyes; that's supposed to be my son, he said to my mother, that's really the biggest disappointment. The fact that my brother was good at volleyball didn't help one jot – all the training, he made a real effort – the disappointment was simply too great for my father. He couldn't stand wimpishness, the wimpishness of my brother and mother, flowery souls, he called them. My father was sporty and harboured sporting ideals, competitive ones; he would have counted competitiveness among his sporting ideals. And luckily I was sporty and my father assumed that I harboured sporting ideals and was competitive, too, which wasn't true, but he didn't realize this at first, so at least I didn't ruin his life by being unsporty. Instead I ruined it with my bandy legs. I inherited them from him; they're not bad on a man or a footballer, but on a girl they look absolutely dreadful; besides, I had spots. I was, however, always good at school; you inherited your ambition from me, my father said, you'll be successful one day, please do me a favour and make something of yourself; in fact I was very ambitious and always received Ones for my homework and in my school reports. I didn't want to be like my brother, who utterly ruined my father's life with his Fours; my father simply couldn't tolerate being disgraced by his own flesh and blood. My brother never managed to lie; I could, even though I never got any Fours; I did, however, earn extra cash on the sly by tutoring younger children – we had very little pocket money – and with my extra cash I went to the cinema on the sly and spent entire days in cafés; I was good at school so I could hide the fact that I was earning cash and spending it in cafés, not to mention cinemas. My father himself loved going to the cinema when he was young; he really loved going to the cinema because at home we children just screamed all day long, me more than my brother, and then when he studied in Berlin, he loved going too. He utterly detested the small provincial town where we first lived, it wasn't cosmopolitan enough for him and the cinema offered the only escape. I liked going to the cinema, too, but I preferred not to say it out loud, instead I said that we had games in period thirteen, which was a lie. There was no period thirteen, school was long finished for the day when I came back late, but nobody noticed. I spent days tutoring younger children, sitting in cinemas and cafés, smoking cigarettes and reading books, and didn't go home until after period thirteen, which didn't exist. At any rate, it was easier for me to lie than my brother; our test results at school had to be signed by a parent, and my mother always said that our father should sign them; in the evening she would tell my father, and my brother couldn't escape. Mum felt bad afterwards when my brother ran from the living room, sobbing and with a bloody nose, and she sobbed the whole time as she heard my father yelling in the living room. Basically she felt bad about having to disappoint my father and about my brother's bloody nose, which was a consequence of this disappointment. My father reproached her, too;

after all, he couldn't keep an eye on everything; of course a mother is to blame if her son is so bone idle that he only manages Fours; his lack of intelligence can't be down to me, my father said, you see my father's an intelligent man, so the failure couldn't be down to him. But perhaps, my father said, the reason he's stupid and idle may have something to do with the fact that my mother was not regarded as particularly intelligent in the family; maybe this was the reason I, at least, was regarded as intelligent, but that was cold comfort to him, because a man wants to be proud of his son, doesn't he. In a proper family, which my father longed for us to be, the father is proud of his son, and my brother ought to have made more of an effort, but he didn't; I can do what I like, it won't work, my brother always said. Anyhow, it wasn't easy to impress our father, because he was very good at everything he did; my father was a good sportsman and scientist, but music, which my brother may have veered towards, was not important; my father would have been pained by such effeminacy in his only son, such daydreaming makes his heart bleed and spoils his mood.

We suddenly felt utterly helpless and awkward and didn't know what to do. My mother stood up; we're sitting here in the dark, she said, switching the light on. I can't see those revolting things any more, she said, instead of her usual, I don't care for them much; I can't see those revolting things any more, and they did look disgusting, the mussels, they gleam when they're freshly cooked, but now they'd dried up and were all wrinkly. They also seemed darker; yellow with green edging and the shells wide open offered an unpleasant sight. I'm feeling bilious, my mother said, and this made complete sense to me even though I didn't know exactly what bilious meant; my mother knew, she was forever suffering from bilious complaints. And we glared at the mussels until my mother fetched from the fridge the wine meant for that evening's celebration. It was a *Spätlese*, a special one; we always drank *Spätlese* on special occasions, and on really special occasions we drank sweet ice wine. The more a wine tastes of liqueur the better quality it is, and this *Spätlese* was bound to be very expensive and high quality, in fact we ought not to have been drinking it before my father arrived home, but we couldn't spend the whole evening staring at the vile mussels, with my mother feeling bilious. She opened the wine and we felt terribly insubordinate. We sat around the dead mussels as if part of some conspiracy and drank father's second-best wine without him, gradually realizing that the mood had been spoiled for all of us; my brother said, this sticky stuff, is this what he considers to be high quality. We couldn't help laughing at my brother's grim expression, and he and I drank as quickly as our mother, only she gets tipsy more quickly; our helplessness and anxiety faded away, and at that point we were fairly sure that he'd had a car accident because he still hadn't come home. As we drank the *Spätlese* our mood became ever more peculiar; we normally drank tea and milk in the evenings, only my father drank beer and sometimes cognac. He always drank cognac while drawing his logical conclusions, a fact we discovered by chance that evening when my brother said, as he fetched the glasses, I loathe that wall unit in the living room, he always starts by pouring himself a cognac from the bar in the wall unit, and then he gets going. He behaved in exactly the same way with me; he'd always go to the bar – the name he gave to the collection of bottles in the middle of the wall unit – and pour himself a cognac before he started asking questions and drawing logical conclusions. My brother couldn't have known that he did the same with me, and I couldn't have known that he did the same with my brother, as he always locked the living-room door and put the key in his pocket; nor could my mother have known, for she was in the hall the whole time. Mum couldn't stand the wall unit, either, in her case because it was new-old German style, and her taste was altogether different, not so solid or weighty, but my father didn't allow them to buy cheap furniture any more. My mother also found the wall unit too dark, she would have preferred it to be a little lighter, a little more friendly-looking, she said, but of course she never mentioned this to my father. He was extremely assured in his taste; he didn't like his taste being questioned. I couldn't bear the wall unit, as I told them that evening, due to my head having been smashed against it on a number of occasions; the handles are positively lethal, I said. The drawer handles were made of turned oak, and protruded dangerously, my mother often banged her knee on them while cleaning; the keys in the doors were no better, brass; I said that the handles and keys on this new-old classical German wall unit were positively lethal, whether they were turned wood or brass. But the handles and keys are nothing, I added without a pause, compared to the panes of bullseye glass, because you spend the entire time trying to avoid going through the bullseye glass; what would have happened if one of us had gone through a pane of glass and broken it doesn't bear thinking about. My brother agreed with me; he, too, found the bullseye glass far worse, more treacherous than the turned-oak handles and brass keys, and he also said that, quite apart from the fact that they're lethal, wall units have no function; I then reminded him of the bar, which does have a function, and my mother reminded my brother and me of the stamp collection, and then, of course, he had to concede that wall units do have a function, ours was full of the stamps that my father had collected for my brother and me, as an investment for the future. There were a number of stamp albums, which on their own you wouldn't have needed an entire wall unit for, but stamps used to arrive in the post roughly every month, always packed up in little packets; my father aimed for completeness, a stamp collection only makes sense and has any value if it's complete, he said. The packets would arrive in the morning when nobody was at home, and had to be paid for on delivery; the invoice would sit in our postbox, indicating how much the stamps cost this time, the striving for completeness had its price, too, and in the afternoon one of us would have to go and collect them. This is ruining me again, your future, my mother said when she saw from the invoice the price she had to pay for our future, but her griping was in jest and she paid for the packet; and thus our stamp collection did become pretty much complete, and the packets started to fill our wall unit completely, which meant it did have a function. In our living room, packed up in little packets, were all the stamps which had been issued in West Germany and the GDR since 1965. Later my father signed up for another deal that went back to the war; our fortune was piled up in the wall unit in the form of a stamp collection which was nearing completion, an all-German and very valuable investment for the future, according to my father. Once my mother called it a rather expensive pleasure, this investment for the future, and my father was stunned by her lack of understanding and proceeded to explain to her the increase in value. She didn't want to know; she said, you may well be right, but they're already quite dear today, these all-German stamps, and then he said, that's what investment means and it will pay back; scrimping on investments makes no sense at all, it's obvious you come from a village where the future is stuffed into a stocking, you'll never be rid of your penny-pinching for as long as you live; my father thought that scrimping on investments was the height of provincialism, and sometimes my mother would reply that her grandmother used to put her money in washing baskets under the bed during the currency crisis and inflation. Then she asked, do you actually know how much they cost, but my father wasn't interested in what they cost because he was at the office when the packets arrived and had to be redeemed at the post office; he laughed, saying, only a fraction of what they'll bring and be worth later on, surely you don't want to scrimp on your children's future, and of course she didn't want that; besides, the stamps gave our wall unit a function. My father also ordered all the accessories for the stamps, the tweezers and magnifying glasses and all

those instruments needed to sort out stamps; they
sat in his desk, and he tried to teach us how to
organize stamps in stamp albums, the system and
technique; he also ordered the catalogue each year,
and we were meant to sort the stamps according to
the catalogue, but we were so stupid with the very
first stamp, so utterly gormless, that he had to
conclude, you've got no sense of the value of a stamp
collection, anybody who's so gormless with the first
stamp cannot be helped, clumsiness and sloppiness
are the enemies of stamp collecting; and he showed
us again, but we weren't able to make any sense of
either the vast quantities of packets or the catalogue.
Then I drove my father up the wall by saying that
all stamps look pretty much the same, don't you
think, because there were so many of them and
there's a big difference between sorting ten stamps
or several years' worth; he was, he said, a passionate
stamp collector, and his dream had always been to
have an all-German stamp collection, it pained him
to see us sabotage this dream with our gormlessness,
and to see our lack of thoroughness and patience in
helping him achieve his dream of all-German
completeness, which after all was an investment for
our future. My father couldn't spend his evenings
and weekends organizing all-German stamps into
these albums for our future; this was our task, a task
which from the outset we'd approached, not with

thoroughness and patience, but with clumsiness and sloppiness, and that's why he couldn't trust us with such an expensive and valuable stamp collection, even though it was meant for us. My father left it until a later date when we'd be able to behave responsibly with our stamp collection and future; the sole result of this was that our wall unit became full of tiny pay-on-delivery packets which my grumbling mother or one of us had to redeem at the post office every month, only to stuff them into one of the drawers afterwards. The shelves of our wall unit were full, too, because my father, who had a keen enthusiasm for completeness, possessed every single issue of *Der Spiegel*, storing them on the shelves of the wall unit, every edition since the currency reform. And to celebrate its anniversary, *Der Spiegel* offered its entire back catalogue for sale, so my father bought every edition, because *Der Spiegel* has been German history since 1948. In the same vein, his first task after our flight to the West was to buy the entire Ziegler, a twenty-volume encyclopaedia of history, on credit. After we arrived in the West a new view of history seemed due and sorely needed; my father received his view of history in twenty volumes and on credit from Herr Ziegler; there was a lot we knew nothing about over there, he said, filling the gaps seamlessly with Ziegler. When my father embarked on something it would be as good as finished, and so the wall unit became full, the unit we hated not just because the complete history threatened us from its lofty shelves; if there was something we didn't know and we asked about and wanted an explanation for, my father would leap up, grab the Ziegler and leaf through it. He'd read the article to himself first, look up references in other volumes – sometimes there'd be three or four volumes open by the end – and my father would painstakingly research whatever we wanted to know in the Ziegler while we became restless. We didn't know what to do in the living room, and our homework never got done by staring at my father as he researched our questions. Then he'd give us a detailed historical explanation because we weren't very well educated historically in our schools, my father said, we were taught a false and superficial view of history, an express education, not thorough and complete, starting at the very beginning, as they did over there, the only problem being that what they taught over there was false, unfortunately, which was one of the reasons for getting out. My father didn't read to us only from the Ziegler, but that's what he mainly consulted to expand our poor historical knowledge; he'd read us several pages until he came to our question, sometimes not even getting that far as he had to read a lot of pages, while we were unable to understand or remember everything because there was no breadth or depth to what we learned at school, it was only bullet points and surface knowledge, i.e. superficial knowledge; all we learned was how to take short cuts and regurgitate. My father realized this as soon as he saw the way we were looking at him as he was reading us the Ziegler; our school system and our mother taught us to take short cuts and regurgitate, so instead of listening with interest to what he was reading out in response to our question, we looked at him impatiently, understanding nothing; all we wanted was a date or a short explanation for our homework, something we could learn by heart and use, not the complete history from the very beginning. We never acquired this thorough Ziegler knowledge, nor were we curious or eager about what the encyclopaedia revealed as we'd been systematically brought up to take short cuts, rather than systematically learning how to think, and that's what my father wanted to teach us when he looked up our questions in the Ziegler. He was determined to fill our gaps, but obviously we didn't want them filled, all we wanted was a short answer. But there aren't and cannot be short answers, and if I could get by at school with my bullet-point, surface knowledge, this was because nowadays, my father said, they gave Ones to us pupils who took the easy route and regurgitated, rather than Fours, which we would have received in the past, when high marks depended on other factors. My father said, in my day your One would have been a Four at most, maybe not even that, and deep down my father thought that even my Ones weren't good enough. What we had to do to get a Three, he said, that would be off the scale these days; my father was an exceptionally good pupil, and my brother often didn't dare come home with his school reports, and to me my father said, well, it looks all right, but these grades are worthless nowadays, and then he'd fetch his reports from the desk and compare them, and if mine was better than his he'd be especially quick to notice the drop in standards, identifying all the things he knew and could do at my age. I could do practically none of those or only very few, because I played piano and read books, and these were of very little value compared to logarithms. Playing piano and reading books won't get an engine started, my father pointed out; he also said, it's useless if you don't understand the difference between necessary and good enough. Unfortunately he was right there. I didn't understand the difference, even though it was very important in our family, as important as it was in logic, for a One was necessary in order to avoid spoiling my father's mood, but it wasn't good enough, and so I generally achieved the standard which was necessary, but not one which was good enough; my brother, on the other hand, failed even to achieve what was necessary. Although it was necessary to come home with Ones, in reality these Ones were worthless – they were phoney Ones – since they'd been given to bullet-point and surface knowledge, and this angered my father, who refused to put up with the lack of education, the express education, in his family, thus the necessary standard was never good enough. In fact I don't ever remember a standard being good enough; it was in the nature of all necessary standards that they weren't good enough, so I played the piano and read books, wasting my intelligence, much to my father's chagrin. Back then, you see, it was assumed that I'd follow in his footsteps and study science; I wouldn't have been able to study piano, as I'd dearly wanted to for years. My father didn't like me playing the piano; stop that tinkling this minute, he'd often say when he came home tired and found me still at the piano, even though he was adamant that my brother and I should play at least one instrument and practise this instrument for an hour a day, and while my brother didn't do an hour's practice, I'd occasionally play for more than an hour and was caught practising by my father in the evening. Such excessive practising aroused his anger and spoiled his mood; in my defence I argued that you couldn't become a pianist with just an hour's practice a day, but my father had an allergic reaction to my playing, it turned his stomach; in a flash I had to jump off the stool, gather my music and shut the piano lid – my father even became allergic to the traces of my practising – and eventually I stopped, after which I spent all day and all night reading. I often fell asleep in front of the TV and had to be carried to bed, where I'd wake again and start reading the moment the door was closed. I was permanently pale from staying up all night. The child doesn't look healthy, my father said; that comes from reading. I secretly borrowed books from our municipal library and hid them, always scared that my father might find them; in a proper family, my father said, there's no need for secrets, and each one of us was terrified of being caught committing a secret crime. Only now were we able to cast off our fears and worries, because it was getting later and later, and we had drunk a bottle of *Spätlese* and all three of us were tiddly. A mere residue of anxiety prevented us from looking at the clock. And we didn't look at the clock until later; before then we said, he must have been in an accident, but an accident can be any number of things, there are accidents and then there are accidents, we said; at this stage we'd ruled out the possibility of a breakdown, because he would have called, it was late after all. After an accident, you go to hospital at least, my brother said, and I said, at least. My mother changed the subject, saying, well, wouldn't it be nice for once to have a Sunday without that Verdi racket, eh; in our house, you see, a Verdi record – at least one – was played every Sunday morning, and my father would whistle along to it; we had to be as quiet as church mice, as quiet as during the sports programme, and we had to stay in the living room and listen to my father whistling along to *Rigoletto* or *Aida* while Mum was cooking the roast, and this lasted until lunchtime; my mother couldn't stand this endless Verdi, as she called it, this substitute for music, she said, this banal growling of the basses. She would close the kitchen door, refusing to come out again until Verdi was finished in the living room, then she'd open the window, albeit inconspicuously, to let out what remained of *Il Trovatore*; after all, my father always said with great satisfaction, Verdi's the only music worth listening to, while my mother tried desperately to avoid the repulsive 'Chorus of the Hebrew Slaves'. For many years the 'Chorus of the Hebrew Slaves' tormented my mother, Verdi in general tormented her, and the torment I suffered was especially cruel, because my father whistled along to it while the record was playing and we weren't ever allowed to leave the living room. On rare occasions we struck lucky and my father would play Mozart, but only *The Magic Flute*, an opera he was able to whistle in its entirety from start to finish without stopping, which gave him a huge appetite for the Sunday roast. My mother couldn't bear Verdi or Sunday roasts, as all week long she had to work and cook and clean and bring up her children; she didn't enjoy spending her Sunday mornings in the kitchen, she said, but my father was never away on Sundays, his business trips lasted from Monday to Friday, so Mum was never once spared Verdi, that musical vermin plaguing our living room, as she put it several times that evening when already quite tiddly, that musical vermin plaguing our living room. And I said, at least you're out of the room, you can hardly hear it, but she said, if that's the choice – Verdi or roast veal – then no thank you, protesting for the very first time in her life. Besides, she pointed out, although Verdi may have been necessary to ensure a happy Sunday, he certainly wasn't good enough; we thought about her bold statement for a while and among all the many requirements necessary to ensure a happy Sunday, we couldn't find a single one which was good enough. We felt the difference between necessary and good enough was as fuzzy as the beauty question; none of us could remember a single Sunday which was even halfway good enough. On Sundays in particular my father loved to expound his notions about a proper family and he began his expounding at breakfast, saying, today we're going to take a drive to here or there; sometimes my brother whined, not again, but then his Sunday would come to a very abrupt end; for my mother it sometimes came to an end at lunch, if she had let the roast dry out – once she even let it burn; on that occasion, however, my father put mercy before justice – but quite often the roast was dry, and then, my father said, his generosity dried up, too. Especially when it was the Christmas goose, then his generosity dried up completely; it was a Hungarian one, that Christmas goose, which my mother had bought cheaply, and because it was cheap it couldn't have been anything other than dry. My father repeatedly tried to explain to my mother that, unlike the Hungarian ones, Polish Christmas geese wouldn't be dry. That didn't make sense to my mother: after all, the Poles were a poor people, so how come their geese wouldn't be dry and tough. My mother didn't really understand how currency exchange worked, she fancied a Polish goose would be leaner than a Hungarian one, because she didn't think the Hungarians looked as hungry; but the cheaply bought Hungarian Christmas goose failed to oblige her by being a fat and meaty goose; on the contrary, it was pathetically dry, bony and tough; that's where the generosity dried up, and with this Hungarian carcass my mother's Christmas was over, just as her Sundays frequently came to an end at lunchtime when she served a dry roast. Occasionally we made it through the afternoon, but generally not much beyond, for one of my father's notions about a proper family dictated that all of us should do something together; mostly we would take a drive somewhere in the car and then go for a walk together, because my father had spent the whole week in the office and was dying for some fresh air at the weekend; but we always had to drive far to find the right fresh air, and when we finally reached our destination, the car park was often full. And my father spent the journey whistling *Rigoletto* and smoking, and that made me feel sick; I always asked him to stop the car, and sometimes he did stop so I could get out and throw up; but he couldn't stop just anywhere, and I still had to be sick, which meant of course that my Sunday was over. It was also over when I said I felt sick because of the smoke and his fast driving; of course I didn't say that *Rigoletto* made me feel sick, too, it was enough to have mentioned the smoke and his fast driving. I only pointed it out once and never again; in any case, by the time we started looking for a parking space Sunday was definitively over, because my mother said that there was also fresh air to be had behind our house, plenty of fresh air, and sometimes we said that behind our house the other children were playing Star Trek; we hardly ever played Star Trek with the other children, because we had to go together as a family to find fresh air in places with full car parks, while behind our house there was not only plenty of car-parking space, but also plenty of fresh air. My father became furious; we had no sense of spending time together as a family, and my mother swiftly demonstrated her good sense by admiring the scenery; behind our house the scenery wasn't as beautiful, besides, we looked at our back garden every day, while my father had the brilliant idea of driving to this beautiful spot with plenty of fresh air. On Sundays my mother switched to wifey mode more than ever, and we found her intolerable, but we didn't dare mention Star Trek again; in fact, on one Sunday afternoon, purely by chance we managed to slip outside and tried to play Star Trek with the other children, but the other children didn't want to play Star Trek with us. We'd never played Star Trek with them before, and if you've never played Star Trek you can't just come along and start playing it when the others are in the middle of their game; my father said that those weren't proper families, they had no sense of family life, only indifference, and so their children play on the street. I wished at once that we had a little more indifference in our family, at least enough to allow us to go to our rooms while my father whistled *Rigoletto*; that was more togetherness than I found appropriate, and anyway when we went out in the afternoons to get some fresh air we generally strolled through the countryside separately, because

Sunday was already over, and I thought we could just as easily have stayed at home. My father talked to my mother about his week at the office, whereas my mother didn't talk to my father about her week at school, because the office was important and worth more than school; sometimes they planned our holidays and decided that we'd go to the sea next year, to Italy, Yugoslavia, Spain or Turkey; over time the distance from home increased. My mother loved the mountains, too, and said, Austria is closer and only half the price; she went on and on about the mountain lakes she'd heard about, and flower meadows appeared before her eyes; she pictured herself carrying armfuls of flowers into a wooden hut, for my mother often longed for village life; and the holiday resorts we always went to in the south looked very un-village-like, nor were there any flower meadows, but instead we had meals in huge dining halls. Although my mother was pleased that she didn't have to cook on holiday, she pointed out that she'd rather cook on holiday than lie in bed sleeplessly above the discotheque again, because in Yugoslavia our bedroom was situated directly above the discotheque, but my father said, if we go to Austria it might rain the entire holiday, and immediately my mother agreed that we should go to the south again, because my father really needed the sun on his holidays. Once, when we were in Turkey, the sun shone only periodically rather than uninterruptedly in the first week, and then we counted ourselves lucky that it shone uninterruptedly in the second week. My mother can't take the sun; she instantly turns red in the sun, whereas my father after being burned goes pretty dark. My mother doesn't like sunburn, she always said, I can't imagine it's healthy to suffer like that, but my father said, you have to get through it, without the sunburn you don't go brown; he drizzled lemon juice over all our sore spots and we were never able to decide whether sunburn was worse with lemon juice or without. My mother said, forget the martyrdom, this is absolute purgatory, but my father said, it helps, and he laughed at us when we fussed; stop making such a fuss, he'd say, and, pain is relative; that, in fact, was true, because my father had hardly any sensitivity to the sun; it's all about strength of character, he said, and my mother seemed not to have much strength of character, indeed she seemed rather weak. Her sensitive skin instantly turned red in the sun, and she spent her holiday in the shade, only because she was such a fusspot, whereas gritting our teeth in our attempts to impress our father, we went into the sun. It didn't work because after the sunburn we turned nowhere near as brown as my father, but at least he couldn't call us fusspots like my mother, who had holed up in the shade; it's always so hot in the south, she moaned, so hot that you don't feel like doing anything during the day. My mother would have loved a nap after lunch, that's what they do here, she said, have a siesta, and get up again when it's cooler; my father thought a nap a waste of holiday, they can enjoy the sun all year round, he said, we don't come all this way south not to take advantage of the sun. And before booking the holidays, my father looked in the brochures and compared the average hours of sunshine per country and per year, and then worked out the probability of enjoying uninterrupted sunshine throughout our stay; that's why he would never go to the mountains, where it can be overcast, and frankly a rainy holiday with my father would have been no fun, which is why on Sunday afternoons, when they were making holiday plans, they always decided to go south to the sea. And my mother secretly brought back a few twigs and grass stalks from our outings, sometimes daisies and bellflowers, too; when my father caught her he just shook his head at this ingrained nostalgia for the countryside, your incurable romanticism, he said; but the twigs and grasses and bunches of flowers rarely survived the journey home because of the traffic, and by the time we arrived home they'd dried out. We always got back in time for the sports programme, though, and it was usually better for my brother and me if our Sunday was already over, otherwise it would be over in dramatic fashion during the sports programme, for my brother and I were intractable in our failure to remember the rules of football or the names of the footballers; I could only remember Uwe Seeler, my brother wasn't much better – he only knew Beckenbauer – and my father despaired; that borders on sabotage, he repeated again and again, and then usually one of us would stammer hopefully, Müller, and the other would stammer speculatively, Mayer; and if Müller or Mayer was not playing in that game then Sunday was definitively over. I remembered Uwe Seeler only because he was the one bald player and easy to spot; the others had hair and all looked the same on television, but my father was able to identify them accurately and he knew who was sitting on the subs bench, too, as well as having a detailed knowledge of the league table. Once, to oblige him, I asked, what's a corner, when he shouted, corner, but he threw me out of the room; actually I was quite happy about this as I was in the middle of reading *Pole Poppenspäler*, and now I had some free time until supper; we didn't play skat that day either, so I had even more time for *Pole Poppenspäler*. When my father was away on business I was allowed to read as much as I wanted, I was also allowed to practise the piano for longer than an hour, or less, even; I could practise the piano as and when I liked, which wasn't the case with my father around, and this fact alone saddened me upon his return, and my mother was sad because my brother had to dash downstairs with the rubbish, including all the flowers and twigs and grasses, so that my father wouldn't catch her wallowing in her ingrained nostalgia for the countryside. My brother had more secrets than ever, the entire basement where we kept the bikes was full of them, but when my father was away on business there were scarcely any secrets between us. Of course we didn't do everything together as in a proper family, we only dealt with the shopping, washing, tidying and those sorts of things more or less together, the things my mother usually did on her own when my father was home, because he despised menial work, and my brother and I went to great pains to ensure that he didn't despise us. Without my father around we often did the menial work together, it was quicker that way and we could talk to each other while doing the chores; for hours we told each other stories, either made up or not, or somewhere in between, which wasn't usual in our family because there were important things and unimportant things, and my father said all the important things, while my mother blabbed to him about all the other important things, and the unimportant things were too unimportant to talk about and that's why we seldom or never talked with my father at home. Now, too, we talked about this and that, as the three of us sat around the table and he didn't come home; we also wondered why we put up with it, just as my father wondered; I'm not going to put up with that, he'd often say when his mood was spoiled, it's sheer tyranny, if that's what a proper family's like then no thank you, all three of us now said, and we said it one right after the other, so that nobody could blab. Mum sometimes said, you've got to see the good sides, too, I mean there are so many good sides to him, and then she said, have a little sympathy for him; but that evening our sympathy vanished and stayed away and never came back. We said, still all three of us, and who'll show us some sympathy; we sounded childish and angry, and we were angry at our mother, too, because our mother always said, just have a little sympathy for him; we did what we could, but that evening, as I said, our sympathy vanished; my brother said, I could do with the odd ounce of sympathy, too, but in our family sympathy didn't come your way for nothing, you had to earn it first. Our father would have given us short shrift if we'd gone and asked him for some cheap sympathy, sympathy for nothing. He'd had to battle his way through life, he didn't get by on the cheap; he'd never once been guilty of the shirking he ascribed to us, not for a single moment, he said, only when you had to battle through life did you see who had real character; endless sympathy is no good, you need to achieve to make an impression. But apparently we weren't cut out for achievement and making an impression; remember all those years ago when you didn't fancy doing that dive, my father said, that would have been one minor achievement at least. We liked going swimming, but we didn't like diving, we liked swimming and going underwater; we liked going to the pool because my father's colleagues and sometimes his boss went too, with their families, and then my father wasn't able to shout at us and could only say, we'll have words later, which is what he said that day, too, when my brother and I were supposed to dive. My brother was slightly braver than me, I used to be a real chicken when it came to diving; even the idea of diving head first from the starting block struck fear and terror in me, though I wasn't so cowardly in other ways; I climbed the highest trees and was always known as the monkey in our family. I was brave when it came to climbing trees – I certainly wasn't a coward – but my father would often tell the story of the father who says to his son standing on a wall, jump, come on, jump, I'll catch you, and the son becomes scared and says, I'm not going to jump, but the father says, don't be scared, I'll catch you, and finally the son does jump, the father steps aside, the son falls and hits the ground, hurting himself badly, and sobs, why didn't you catch me; the father laughs and says, trust no one, remember that, not even your own father. I was never able to laugh at this joke as my father wanted me to, it was a cruel joke, the laughter stuck in my throat, and unfortunately I couldn't help thinking of this very joke whenever I was about to jump into the water. And I was never able to bring myself to jump into the water, especially not head first, even when my father was already in the water and said, but I'm here, that didn't help, the fact that he was there; he couldn't have caught me in the water, and I was certain I would drown. I've only dived head first once in my entire life, once and never again, but my father couldn't cope with the humiliation of having cowardly children, who failed the courage test miserably, and so he said, if you dive from the three-metre board I'll give you five marks. My brother climbed up to the three-metre board in a flash, but once there his courage deserted him, and he climbed back down again. My father turned ashen-faced from sheer disappointment – that was a bad sign – my brother started howling and my father said he'd even dived from the five-metre board, so my brother climbed back up, jumped finally and received the five marks after all; so, was it really that bad in the end, my father asked him; my brother was so proud that he replied, absolutely not, and I felt ashamed at being a coward so I climbed up, too, and dived in head first. It was terrible. My head and back just hurt, the pressure in my ears ached badly, too, because my ears are so useless and hurt even if I go under just two metres, and when I did that dive I must have gone three or four metres under; I thought I'd never get back to the surface. I was so overcome by earache – even as a child I had regular ear infections – I thought my ears were going to burst, and I could no longer tell what was above and what below, with the pain in my ears I completely lost my orientation underwater, and then all the air went out of me; I'm going to die, I thought, because I'm never going to get back up again. After an age I finally made it back to the surface. I was sick at the side of the pool due to the pain, and because the dive had been so terrible, and my father asked me the same question: was that really so bad; horrible, I said, really horrible, and my father said, do it again, you need to jump again straight away. But I didn't, even though he said I had no strength of character. I didn't want the five marks if it meant I had to dive again; my father didn't want to pay me the five marks for the dive itself, rather – as I thought at the time – he wanted to pay me for having enjoyed it, or for me saying that I'd enjoyed it; I said I'd rather have no strength of character than jump again and say I enjoyed it, when in fact it's horrible.

We forfeited all our father's sympathy, we said that evening, also saying that any sympathy we might have felt for our father had vanished; we even said that the sole reason our sympathy had vanished was because any sympathy he'd had for us had also vanished long ago; the fact that we were always there, ruining his life, had drained all sympathy from him, as he sometimes said; I wish you weren't born, he once remarked, adding that he deeply regretted having fathered first me – by accident – and then my brother, who had been planned, but who he regarded as a mistake, a disastrous one when he looked at the result: his son a complete and utter failure, which he blamed on my mother and the school system which had relentlessly mollycoddled him in the most irresponsible way; while from the outset he'd hated my obduracy, my unappealing side; that evening my mother said that from the outset my father hadn't shown the slightest sympathy for my unattractiveness. The first time he saw me, apparently, he cried out in horror, it's a monkey, tearing his hair out because there was no way that ugly thing could be his daughter, let alone the son he was meant to have had. I was very ugly when I was born, my mother said, but that didn't bother her; I didn't notice, she said; she didn't realize until the midwife consoled her by saying, don't worry, it can all change; Mum found me exceptionally pretty all the same and loved me straight away, even though she could see what the midwife had meant when she said, don't worry, it can all change. I was covered in hair from top to bottom, there was black hair over my entire body – apparently even my face was hairy like a monkey's – my entire body right down to my toes; I was so plug-ugly when I was born that my father was disgusted by the sight of me; my mother always said she found me exceptionally lovely straight away, only later did she notice that I looked like a black monkey. The hair fell out after a few days, and from then on I looked like all other babies, but it was too late for my father, who had already formed a negative impression of me, there was no way of salvaging this impression; my father is a good-looking man, you see, and he felt aggrieved that he of all people should have fathered a little black monkey. My father's hair grows quickly, he needs to shave twice a day to avoid a shadow on his chin, and he was especially proud of his hair, because other men went bald, but my father had such thick black hair that he didn't have to worry about going bald; he thought bald men plain silly, apart from Uwe Seeler, who he didn't find quite so silly. Whenever someone said to him after I was born, she's just like her father, he'd go mad; apparently he went straight from the clinic to get drunk, unable as he was to cope with his daughter's ugliness while sober; my mother didn't notice any ugliness, she said, but he showed not the slightest sympathy from the outset. Apparently my father said how ashamed he felt to have such a monkey for a daughter, and was inconsolable that a handsome person like him could be cursed with such an ugly child; in fact my unappealing side, as he often said, became more pronounced as time went on. Whereas other children were cute and clean, I was forever filthy; they dressed me in clean clothes, but the moment they tried to take me out in a clean coat, I spoiled it; I incessantly puked up the fresh and delicious food they fed me, and while other parents wheeled their rosy, cute-looking children in pushchairs through the village and castle gardens, my mother had to turn back in a hurry, because I'd puked up my entire lunch; they used to say, no matter what you give this child, she pukes it up again immediately, but the truth was – terribly unappealing, I know – I waited until the very moment my mother sat me in the pushchair and was about to go to the castle gardens before puking up, not a second earlier, which meant that everyone could see me puking up my entire lunch. I'd bring up my entire lunch in public, whereas other children would do their burps at home behind closed doors, and right after being fed. I never burped to order after being fed, and I didn't just do one burp, either, but many burps, and not until I'd been put in a clean coat; I never puked up twice on the same coat, my mother said, besides I howled from morning to night, and Mum could have fed me from morning to night; I must have been such a glutton, no sooner had I downed a bottle of formula than I'd start howling again for more, even though I hadn't puked up the first bottle yet. I was only quiet, my mother said, when I had the bottle of formula in my mouth, and hence I became a very chubby baby. There are photos of how chubby I was, so chubby I couldn't move, all the same I continued to howl the second my bottle was empty; my father, thank God, was studying at the time, he was renting a room in Berlin and only came home at the weekends, but he couldn't bear those weekends, because I didn't just howl from morning to night, but from night to morning, too: all night, every night. My parents put my cot in the room furthest away from theirs and closed the doors, but still neither of them could sleep a wink, my howling must have been so ghastly; my mother told me that my father said, she's not a monkey, she's the devil incarnate, so my mother spent her weekends comforting and placating my irate father; he was not to be comforted or placated, however, particularly not at night, as he couldn't sleep through my howling; his devilish child, this spawn of Satan, enraged him so much that once he picked me up and threw me against the wall. My father later said that this was the first time

I was quiet, and I asked, what happened then, but my parents couldn't remember what happened then. I even limped like the devil himself, forever dragging one leg behind me, from the moment I could walk, because there was a problem with the way my hip bone had developed, which of course nobody could anticipate and detect in a small child before they could walk. My mother was pleased that my father wasn't at home the whole time, for my howling was unreasonable; my grandmother, too, thought that this child wasn't appealing and cute like the other children who were all pretty and clean, and who didn't howl, certainly not all night long, especially not the girls; puking and howling are unseemly; boys might do those things from time to time, although my brother was one of those cute babies, he never brought up his food and never howled, nor was my brother such a glutton. He was gentle. My father pitied his gentleness and his permanent cuteness enraged him, while he found it lacking in me. And my parents assumed their unappealing daughter would never find a husband, whereas my brother's girly nature – he even wanted to wear dresses when he was little – made my father suspicious from the outset, my mother said. My brother was blond and rosy and always smiling, a child with a permanent smile, apparently; from the outset my father found my brother's smile peculiar, and my father always said, that's meant to be my son; I was supposed to have been his son, and my father showed no sympathy for the fact that I wasn't his son; I was too ugly and unappealing to be his daughter, I was my father's monkey, whereas my brother was my mother's golden boy; she saw nothing peculiar about his smile, just as she'd seen nothing monkey-like about me and my initial hirsuteness. Only later did she realize that her daughter was a little devil; she worried a lot about both her children, but showed sympathy, too; my mother always showed sympathy for everybody. And that evening, even though she was being insubordinate for the first time in her life, she tried to persuade us to show some sympathy for our father, which we absolutely refused to do because our sympathy had vanished, it never having been aroused in my father, as my mother said, but forfeited from the outset.

Even when Mum said, he had it hard, your father, this didn't change our minds; we said to our mother, don't cop out now, you were being so brave; of course we knew that my father had come from a poor background and had to battle his way upwards, which he managed to do solely by virtue of his huge talent and intelligence; it's hard to do what he did, my mother said, who had it easier; she didn't come from the very bottom and so didn't have to make it the whole way up. When her father died she still had a house, although she was heavily in debt and had to fork out for the mortgage as well as her brothers' studies; both my mother's brothers became musicians as they'd wanted to, and as my mother had wanted to as well, but she quickly became a teacher, while my father wanted to become a scientist and study mathematics, coming as he did from the very bottom and out of wedlock, in the village where his mother wove baskets and knitted jumpers for other people. My grandmother was a very poor woman, and was a constant embarrassment to my father as she had so little to give him, nor could he take her anywhere; I can't be seen anywhere with you, my father said later, when he was already on the verge of being promoted. He didn't have it easy with his mother, she lived in a dingy and grubby place, she only had a single room and the kitchen smelled as it does in poor people's houses, because it *was* a poor person's house, and my father was always angry with her; later, whenever he visited the village, he preferred to stay at the inn rather than at his mother's, even though they had no running water. My mother and I used to stay with my mother's mother, and my father and brother stayed at the inn rather than with my father's mother, who we always called the other grandmother because she was poor, whereas our proper grandmother wasn't poor; she had her own house, and everyone in the village knew her and greeted her, whereas almost nobody knew or greeted the other grandmother, who remained a stranger, a foreigner after she came to Germany. And there was another reason why my other grandmother was called the other grandmother: in family photos she always stood to one side, on the periphery, always a gap between her and the rest of the family. My mother reminded us that it wasn't easy for my father; his mother and his background were huge liabilities, in comparison to the trivial liability on my grandmother's house when my grandfather died; my father did what he could to paper over his background, but it wasn't easy, for my other grandmother was tremendously proud of her brilliant son and clung to him wherever possible. Whenever I visited her she would cry, saying how proud she was that my father had made his way from the bottom to the top. I was very attached to my other grandmother, and my father was very attached to his mother, too; to see her living in the village in such poverty broke his heart, a woman who nobody apart from the simple villagers knew or greeted; your other grandmother is a simple woman, my mother would tell us, and because she was a simple woman she was desperate to receive letters; my mother used to write to her mother once a week, she always wrote to her mother on Sunday evenings, whereas my father couldn't write to his mother; he was a very busy man, and couldn't do that as well; he didn't have the time or energy to do everything, and he couldn't stand being clung to. It's hard enough coming from a poor background and making your way up in the world, you need to use your fists to escape a background like that, you can't allow your background to cling and stick to you; my father would churn inside at the thought of it, he couldn't eat at his mother's house, either, because it wasn't clean or inviting; so untidy, my father said, but there was one occasion when he couldn't avoid it. His mother had said to my mother, you never eat here, you only ever eat there, by which she meant my proper grandmother's, where we always ate when we were in the village, because my father found her place inviting and tidy. And his own mother was offended that we never ate at hers; she said to my mother, he behaves as if he's ashamed; my mother understood – she understood everything – and finally my father agreed to eat at his mother's if she asked someone else to cook: there was no way he was going to eat at hers if she did the cooking herself, he said. In fact she not only paid for the food but the cook, too, so just for once we ate at hers and she was delighted; she was so excited and nervous with delight that she couldn't keep her hands still; my father couldn't bear it when she couldn't keep her hands still. Keep your hands still, he said, but she was too excited about our visit, and after keeping her hands still for barely five minutes, she couldn't keep them still any longer. All her life she'd had to work very quickly with her hands and these rapid movements had made her hands independent; she'd keep them still for barely five minutes, then her fingers would start up again, executing these work movements independently. Eventually my father's patience snapped, and the cook who my other grandmother had hired was no longer good enough to avoid the mood being spoiled. It's impossible to eat here, my father said in a strop because once more he felt ashamed at his mother, who'd led a menial life and had never been able to shake it off, no matter how many times he'd told her to keep her hands still instead of fidgeting. And then he stopped going to hers, whereas I liked going to my grandmother's, because although she was unable to keep her hands still, she did something which never happened in our family, it was forbidden – the other grandmother, they used to say, spends hours staring out of the window. I didn't really understand what there was to disapprove of; I wanted my grandmother to teach me how to stare out of the window for hours, and I liked going to her place; when I was at my grandmother's we did nothing at all. In our house doing nothing didn't exist; it was absolutely imperative that everybody was doing something, all the time;

when I went to cafés later on, I merely carried on in
secret with what I'd picked up from my other grandmother: doing nothing. I never thought my
grandmother was a simple woman; I thought she
was an extraordinary woman, because she was
capable of doing nothing, whereas everybody else
was always doing something; your mother is an
extraordinary woman, I'd often say to my father;
he felt flattered, and then said, look at me, nothing
comes from nothing. Clearly, he didn't understand
what I meant. In any case, he resented her for her
menial life and for the fact that she couldn't keep
her hands still as a consequence of those years when
she'd had to graft so that her son could reach the
top. He was very attached to her, however, and was
so distraught when she died that my mother thought
he'd gone crazy with pain; he mourned his mother
and tore his hair out; he holed up in the bedroom,
locking himself in, and refused to come out for days.
When he did come out he swore that his mother
would have the loveliest grave in the whole village;
he made all the arrangements for this lovely grave,
which wasn't easy because we were in the West and
the village in the East. But he managed to arrange
for the most splendid grave in the whole village; he
invited the entire village to the funeral, everybody
who was anybody, and reserved the restaurant in the
town hall for a meal that nobody was going to forget

in a hurry. He made a precise note of who came to
the funeral and who didn't, and thank God almost
everybody came; there were more than a hundred
people at his mother's funeral, more than had ever
known or greeted her, and the grave lies in a lovely
spot, not too close to the perimeter, under trees, not
in the part of the cemetery for poor people; it's the
only grave with a gold-leaf inscription – my father
ordered gold leaf specially from the West because
there was no gold leaf over there. He could not rest
until his mother's grave was the only one with gold
leaf, and only then did he find peace – apart from
with me. I didn't come to the funeral; he never forgave
me for not coming, you of all people, he reproached
me, you of all people, and he reproached me for
being stubborn and cold-hearted, he had no
sympathy; in our family I was always known as the
stubborn and cold-hearted one, and my stubbornness
and cold-heartedness, which developed from my
unappealing nature, were in evidence yet again when
I refused to go to my grandmother's funeral, to a
place I'd always enjoyed going and where I felt happy.
My father never forgave me for this act of spite and
irreverence, as he called it. But he couldn't force me,
because I'd come of age; my grandmother died at
the very moment when I came of age, just a few days
afterwards; and when I came of age my stubbornness
and cold-heartedness really showed, my father said,

but unlike in the past, before I'd come of age, now there was nothing he could do. He couldn't beat the stuffing out of me; I'll beat the stuffing out of you, he'd have said in the past, I'll give you what for, and I really would have been given what for if he'd beaten the stuffing out of me. My mother would have stood with my brother in the hall by the living-room door, while my father locked the door behind him and fetched a cognac from the bar in the wall unit, the key to the living-room door in his trouser pocket as ever, and my father would have tried to identify the reasons for my stubbornness; could you explain it to me, he'd have asked, and I wouldn't have been able to, because I wasn't able to explain anything if my father yelled at me, and so I'd have been given what for. The more insistently he harangued me, the more stubborn I became, refusing to say a word, all speech abandoning me in one fell swoop. I never knew what to say when my father said, answer me for God's sake; just once, when I was a child, I managed an answer, but it was the wrong one, and wrong answers incensed my father, then he really gave you what for. Since then I've never managed a single answer when my father says, answer me for God's sake, I asked you a question, what have you got to say to me. Out of sheer disappointment he'd have drunk another cognac, leaving me to wonder what I might break if I jumped from the first-floor balcony, but because of the neighbours the windows and balcony door were of course closed, and I couldn't escape. Now my father would have looked completely wild, because I hadn't answered him, he'd have asked me again and again, haranguing me, but ultimately he wouldn't have been able to help himself and he'd be forced to punish my stubbornness, since no understanding or answer had been forthcoming. My father would have said, I'm not going to put up with that, you don't do that with me, and he'd have drunk another cognac and finally said, take your hands away from your face; after the second cognac I'd have already put my hands to my face, hidden my face in my hands – I didn't want my father to hit me in the face – and I'd have said, please, not my face; my father would have said, for God's sake take your hands away from your face, it would have made him livid that I hadn't taken my hands away from my face, it makes me furious, he said again and again, I'm not going to put up with it, but I never took my hands away, he had to remove them himself, both of them, he had to grip both of my hands in his left so he could hit my face with his right and that really made him furious. My stubbornness; he tried to use violence to knock the stubbornness out of me, just as he tried to use violence to knock the wimpishness out of my brother. All my stubbornness was trying to achieve, however, was to avoid flying head first through the bullseye glass; it would have been a catastrophe to fly head first through the bullseye glass, I'd have cowered under his blows, fallen to the floor without saying a word, and I'd have whimpered that he should stop; no, no, I'd have said if my father had started kicking me in the head with his clogs, but my stubbornness would have been absolute. Only later, in my room, where I'd have been locked, would the words return, wicked and vengeful words lacking all understanding. Whenever my brother was locked in his room he always sang loudly, he always sang, always the same song, a folk song, '*Hänschen klein*', which put my father in an even fouler temper; often my brother was hauled out of his room again, but my father couldn't knock the folk song out of him; he could knock the wimpishness out of him, but not the folk song; he severely reproached my mother because of this; my mother said, but I'm doing my best, don't be so hard on them, and my father said, I'm not putting up with it, they're not going to do that with me, they should know me better. We'd got to know our father very well over many years, but when my grandmother died he had to stop because I'd come of age; of course, he didn't speak to me for several weeks after the funeral, he refused to speak to me till I'd apologized for my behaviour, and every day my mother came into my room and said, go on, apologize. She couldn't cope when people didn't speak to each other. But I could cope, because in the evenings I was able to read instead of having to play skat; nobody spoke to me, anyhow, because if my father wasn't speaking to me then the other two weren't allowed to, either; they only spoke to me secretly when he was away. My brother always apologized that same evening, so we all spoke to him, whereas I rarely apologize straight away; sometimes I didn't apologize at all, but sometimes I apologized when my mother said, go on, apologize, can't you see how this pains me. Although I could see how my behaviour pained her, I spent months reading books in my room in the evenings and doing nothing. Sometimes I'd wonder what I'd done, and when I remembered I'd wonder what was so bad about it, but when I missed the funeral, I realized straight away what was bad about *that*. Even then I didn't go, however much that meant betraying my family. In the past, on the other hand, I seldom knew what I'd done wrong. Sometimes I asked. I soon realized this question wasn't a good idea, this question drove my father into a blinding rage, and then he certainly gave me what for; afterwards, when I was in my room, he used to come in and say, now you've got time to think about it. My father could always spot and condemn my wickedness, even when I was totally unaware of it; he showed me how wicked

I was, making it very clear, just as he showed my brother what a wimp he was, making that perfectly clear, too. My brother also wondered what he might break if he jumped from the first-floor balcony, he said that evening; when I'm in a closed room, he said, I'm always drawn to the window, I can't help but be drawn to windows in closed rooms, I always want to jump out of the window, I'm obsessed by this urge. My mother fetched another bottle of *Spätlese* and we carried on drinking. At this point she said, I'm to blame for it all; she always said that, she always took the blame completely, adding, I did it all wrong, and we had to comfort her and say, absolutely not, you didn't do anything wrong, but she said, I'm a wreck; caught between you two and your father I've been ground down to exhaustion. And we were worried that she might sit down at the piano and play Schubert songs, which she was particularly wont to do when she thought she was to blame for everything, or after a domestic scene when my father would slam the door behind him and leave; then she was to blame because my father couldn't bear her pedantry any longer, her stinginess. He'd drive off and not come back until the middle of the night, always after they'd tried to complete their tax return; Mum couldn't do the tax return on her own because she needed bills and receipts, which my father didn't keep because he was generous rather than a nit-picker; and my mother would calculate that we couldn't afford this or that, but my father calculated that he couldn't afford her nit-picking any more; my father didn't scrimp on his generosity on business trips, not with himself, nor with others he met while away and who he'd automatically pay for; out of generosity he'd always pay the bill, and my mother would say, these bills are huge; my father always chucked away the receipts for these bills and never calculated his expenses; he refused to calculate expenses, he would have felt ashamed to do so with the firm. They were both irritated by these discarded expenses; my father would say to my mother, you're so pernickety, and we'd hear them argue, which was rare in our house, because my mother loved harmony and hated arguing; usually she'd give in, so we'd only hear our parents arguing loudly when they filled in the tax return, and also when my father bought Japanese shares. The Japanese firms had a tendency to file for bankruptcy the instant my father put all his money into the shares; my mother took against Japanese shares, she was prejudiced against them since the first bankruptcy; but as soon as another financial adviser visited us and started talking up Japanese shares, my father would offer him *Spätlese*, and after a few bottles of *Spätlese* he'd put all our money into Japanese shares once more. On several occasions all our money was lost from one day to the next and practically overnight, although this didn't stop my father, who was very popular with the financial advisers, from buying Japanese shares the next time. We haven't even paid back all our debts, my mother said, how do you imagine we're going to pay our debts back, and she'd also say, wouldn't it be a dream just to be able to go into a shop and buy a dress; even when my father had climbed the career ladder from the bottom to near the top she continued to imagine what a dream it would be to be able to afford a blouse without fretting over the cost, to be frivolous, she said. But her stinginess didn't allow for such frivolity; my mother always bought our clothes in end-of-season sales, for herself, my brother and me; another special offer, my father would sneer when she showed him a new purchase – a skirt or a jumper – which she had indeed bought at a reduced price; she never dared tell him how cheap it really was, however, as my father would have felt ashamed. When she said, reduced from seventy to thirty, my father said, I'm not going out with you in that reject; my parents rarely went out because of the cut-price rejects my mother always wore. My father, on the other hand, was not only quite a bit younger than my mother, he also wore made-to-measure suits, from day one; only the best was good enough for him once he'd secured the job at his firm. You can spot off-the-peg clothing from miles away, my father said, and whenever my mother wore a new dress he immediately spotted that it was another reject. You don't have any style, he said; my mother agreed that she didn't have any style, how could I have any style when I need to ensure that we have enough, while you're throwing heaps of money out the window; but my father said, it's not heaps, and, I can't help it if you're stingy, and then the door would slam and my father rushed out, coming back in the early hours, drunk. On those evenings Mum would always sing Schubert songs, having first said, I'm to blame for it all, and the mood was grim: my mother sobbing at the piano and the entire flat shrouded in melancholy. That's why when my mother said, I did it all wrong, we were worried that she'd start on the Schubert songs again; whenever my mother said, I did it all wrong or I'm to blame for it all, then that's what usually happened, and she'd add afterwards that she was old and ugly and dull – a Plain Jane – and not sophisticated enough for my father. He desperately needed her to be sophisticated. The men all brought their wives along to firm dos, apart from my father, who couldn't bring my mother because she wasn't sophisticated enough, and because of the special offers and rejects she wore; she didn't understand the etiquette, either, and the one time he did take her along, she embarrassed him horribly. At the very start of the evening my mother was asked whether she'd like a martini, and she said, yes, please, and then she was asked how she'd like her martini, would she like it dry, and she said I only know wet martini, and my father felt utterly humiliated that such a worldly man as himself should be fated to have a wife who didn't know what a dry martini was; my parents never invited people to our house for my father's fear of shattering the positive impression he'd made at work with his efficiency, natural charm and intelligence. Just imagine if my father's boss, who regrettably he'd never been able to invite over, had asked for a martini, and my mother hadn't known what a martini was, thinking that a Cinzano Rosso was a martini, and had served my father's boss a glass of Cinzano Rosso instead; my father's positive impression would have been shattered in the boss's eyes. I can't take the risk, my father said, when my mother said how she'd missed having guests since our arrival in the West, because there hadn't been the right sort of people; nor had there been the right sort of friends around for my brother and me; they came from poor families and so weren't right for us because they wouldn't have had proper table manners. You could tell their poor backgrounds from both how they spoke and the way they looked, in particular that long hair of theirs; my father said, don't let me catch either of you with such a mop of hair. We always had very short hair, my brother and I; for many years people thought I was a boy and said, come on, be a gentleman and pick up the lady's bag for her; if a lady ever dropped anything everybody would look straight at me to bend down, because with my short hair I had to be a gentleman. My brother and I visited the barber's regularly; our heads were shaved from front to back with clippers; my mother would console me, hair grows more nicely if you cut it regularly; I found, however, that it grew better if you let it grow and I wanted to have long hair like my friend, whose poor background you could spot at once on account of her long hair. My other friend wasn't right for me, either, because she was hideously nouveau riche. My parents said that being nouveau riche didn't turn you into a cultured person. This nouveau riche friend of mine was allowed to eat ice cream from the ice-cream van, as much and as often as she wanted, and ice cream from the ice-cream van was not cultured. In any case, my father didn't like coming home in the evening to find other children there, and so my friends, as well as my brother's, always had to leave before supper; it was barely worth them coming at all because my brother and I had to have finished our homework by the time my father came home in the evening, besides our one hour's piano practice, no more and no less. Our friends wouldn't have known what to do in that time, because they did their homework later, in the evening, when we were watching television and playing skat, because we were a proper family and did things together in the evenings, whereas my friends, without exception, didn't come from proper families where they enjoyed things together. Actually I never met anyone who came from a proper family; I was forever meeting people who, without exception, didn't come from proper families, rather from families where the children did their homework in the evenings when their parents had guests or went to the cinema, which as far as I can remember my parents never did. Once a month we'd go to a concert together; we had a subscription, and all senior employees had the same concert subscription as us; my mother was delighted, she loved the concerts, and couldn't stop praising the quality of the music. I'm so starved, she'd say, and we always listened to first-rate international symphony orchestras from London, Tokyo and Philadelphia; the programmes, too, were also well put together; balanced, my mother called them. Haydn would be followed by a modern piece, and then some Brahms after the interval. The applause at the end of these concerts always went on and on until they played an encore, and the encores usually consisted of a brash piece, wild even, mostly another modern composition, but short, which pleased my mother greatly as she wasn't especially fond of this modern music. For me, she said, art finished at the end of the nineteenth century, she even found Mahler a bit odd; I'm not especially fond of Mahler, my mother said on many an occasion, but they never played Mahler at the concerts, and the modern stuff was kept tastefully short because the programmes were balanced. I didn't get to know modern music at these concerts, in short bursts, but from listening to it secretly on the radio, and from the radio I gained the impression that music and mathematics were not so dissimilar, but closely related, they went hand in hand, I told my mother. My mother didn't like twelve-tone music, however, it doesn't have the same harmony, she said; she preferred harmonious music, but not when it went dum-dee-dum-dee-dum like Verdi, who she didn't rate as a serious composer. My father didn't really look forward to these concerts; not again, he'd say, but he had to go along because of the senior employees who milled about in the interval with their drinks; he was always delighted when the concert had finished, and he'd duly said hello to all the senior employees; in fact my father would have been happy to leave after the interval, and he did leave early on a few occasions, but then his colleagues noticed the empty seat. With a subscription you keep the same seat for years, and senior employees greet each other not only in the interval, but also in the concert hall; my father stopped leaving after the interval and saw these concerts through to the end, so that everybody realized that he saw things through to the bitter end. Another reason my father disliked these concerts was that he knew he didn't want to be a senior employee, but a top one; his mind had been set on the top the very first day he joined the firm and he executed the pursuit of this goal not gradually and with patience, but extremely rapidly; indeed, he carried out his plan at the highest speed possible and he considered his attendance at these subscription concerts purely as a means to an end. And that evening my mother suspected that as soon as my father was promoted the subscription would be cancelled. I'm delighted for him, my mother said, but no one seriously believed that he'd ever go to another subscription concert, because he'd now conquered the senior-employee stage, and my mother said that what followed the subscription concerts was the dry-martini stage, the drinks stage; that's what she saw in store for herself. That evening, however, as she was no longer stable on her feet and also insubordinate for the first time in her life, she let slip that she'd definitely prefer the subscription concerts to the drinks stage; I've played along, she said, by which she meant ever more expensive cars and holidays to ever more un-village-like resorts instead of Austrian mountain lakes with plenty of meadows and flowers. And in fact, shortly before leaving on his business trip – which was almost certainly the last stop on his way to promotion – my father had announced that he was looking to cancel his subscription; instead he intended to go to Bayreuth in the summer; all his life he'd misjudged Wagner, and that was a mistake – to misjudge Wagner – so now he intended to correct this mistake. My mother put Bayreuth and the dry drinks and the ever more expensive cars in the same bracket, because she'd never cared in the least for Wagner or dry drinks; that evening she said, I've played along with everything, but at some point it has to stop, by which she meant it stopped at Wagner and the dry drinks; in truth it had already stopped with the *Spätlese*, we replied, but she contradicted us, she really loved the subscription concerts; they were what my mother called classical harmony and she believed in classical harmony. She may not have been religious, but she did believe in classical harmony, in the dominant and subdominant; my mother loved it when we sang quodlibets together; although he came after Brahms, my mother thought that Hindemith was the only composer more skilled in the use of counterpoint; she loathed atonal counterpoint, it hurts my ears, she said, and was happy that the concerts were balanced and that the modern pieces were short, whereas I always felt the modern element of the subscription concerts was a bit pathetic in its balance-inducing brevity. I find classical harmony, with its dominants and subdominants, extremely suspect, I said; I had the suspicion that composers merely stuffed everything into this harmony; those poor voices, I said to my mother, they're being forcibly stuffed into the harmony; but my mother shouted out, no way, harmony's got nothing to do with force, and she talked of coherence and consonance, which didn't exist in twelve-tone music; I said, twelve-tone music equals pure control. My mother tried to get me to appreciate the Schubert songs, but without success; her attempts to push Schubert on me were in vain. I already knew that Schubert used enharmonic modulations, yet my mother never once succeeded in getting me to like the Schubert songs or even appreciate them. No sooner had my mother sat at the piano and started to sing a Schubert song from *Winterreise* than the hairs on my arms, indeed all over my body, would stand on end, because my mother could only sing Schubert songs with a broken voice, on the verge of crying; no sooner had she sat at the piano and started playing Schubert songs than tears would appear, which I called my mother's Schubert tears; maybe it wasn't the Schubert songs but the Schubert tears which made the hairs on my arms stand on end, I used to think, and that evening

I was relieved she didn't go to the piano. Having said that at some point it had to stop, however, she didn't know what would happen if it did stop, because until that evening she'd always thought it had to go on. My brother, meanwhile, was happy that these subscription concerts were going to stop; the concerts were pure torment for him, he said; we had to sit still and the top button of his shirt tormented him, and the music went straight over his head. We'd always go to the concerts very well dressed, the four of us in our best clothes; my father never failed to point out that my mother didn't have any best clothes, only rejects, which spoiled his mood; in this spoiled mood he would look at my brother and me to see whether we, at least, were sufficiently well dressed, then he'd say to my brother, no, you can't leave your top button open, do your button up, and if my brother said, but it itches and scratches, he'd say, those are just your tics, for my brother was sensitive about certain things, one of which was itchy and scratchy closed collars. As soon as he was made to fasten the top button on his shirt my brother would start twisting and stretching his neck this way and that; my father, with his mood already spoiled by the rejects my mother had put on, never failed to notice if my brother tried to slip into the concert with his top button undone; he didn't have a chance, my brother, he had to fasten his top button

immediately, because open collars look sloppy; and
if my father's mood was particularly spoiled, he
really gave my brother what for, and he'd be forced
to wear a tie or bow tie over the fastened button;
from that moment all music went straight over his
head and his tics wouldn't leave him alone the entire
evening; he'd sit in the concert and twist and stretch
his head this way and that because of the torment;
my father, who couldn't show his despair and bitter
disappointment at a subscription concert, felt
humiliated, for everybody could see how my brother
was afflicted by his tics. Over time my brother started
to have difficulties swallowing; as soon as he fastened
his top button he could hardly swallow a single
mouthful without making a peculiar guttural sound
with his throat. This noise could drive my father up
the wall; in our family my brother was likened to
Christian Buddenbrook; leave him, my mother
begged, when my brother's coughs and throat-
clearing got my father's goat, as he put it, but my
father couldn't leave him; I don't want a Christian
Buddenbrook in my family, he said, and wouldn't
tolerate it; my brother didn't want to be a Christian
Buddenbrook, either, he merely didn't want to fasten
his top button. This is how odd habits start, my
father said; there was no question of leaving his top
button undone. My father was convinced that this
is how it all started, and that with his shirt collar

open my brother was even more like that oddball Christian Buddenbrook. Music thus went over my brother's head and he was delighted when Mum said, at some point it has to stop, although she meant Wagner and the martinis rather than the concerts. All the same I asked my mother, why do the subscription concerts have to stop, if you like them so much; this was a highly insubordinate question, and suddenly we felt light-headed from the *Spätlese* and insubordination, because, after all, my mother couldn't just wander off to subscription concerts while my father was stirring dry martinis; there was nowhere my mother could have wandered off to in the evenings, except the occasional parents' evening she had to attend out of duty; she kept these parents' evenings very short so she could be back home again soon, and when Mum was on a class trip the household routinely fell apart; any absence of my mother from the household, however short, led to the household falling apart altogether. Your father's like a little child, she'd say on her return from a class trip, when she noticed the charred smell that hung in our flat whenever my father had to take on the housework. My brother and I had eaten the charred dinner, acting as if nothing were wrong, but it was difficult, because we could rarely identify what the dinner was. My mother's absence on a class trip signalled a far greater disaster for the household than her being ill, because with a temperature of forty degrees she could still look after the household, but she couldn't while away on a class trip, whereas my father was totally incapable, and even when my mother had to attend her parents' evenings, he was as helpless as a little child. She would prepare the dinner in advance, but still she had to keep the parents' evenings as short as possible; even the shortest absence posed a threat to the household, and thus we'd reached the height of insubordination that evening when I said, why do the subscription concerts have to stop; I could have just as easily said that our entire household has to stop. In a way both these statements amounted to the same thing: the sticking together in our household didn't survive my mother being absent for a minute; it all fell apart immediately. Once, when my mother was in hospital, my father was keen to bring her back home after barely a week; absolutely out of the question, the doctor said, he couldn't be held responsible for the consequences, but my father said, the family's falling apart, did he want to be held responsible for that; eventually the doctor said that he, too, had a family, and agreed to let my mother out and back to her family. In that one week so much menial work and washing had piled up that my mother barely managed to get all the washing and ironing and cleaning done, but she gritted her teeth and set about the work.

Pyelonephritis is not a subscription concert, however, and my father only accepted my mother's absence from the household for a week because pyelonephritis is not exactly pleasurable, whereas the subscription concerts were pure pleasure for my mother. My father would never have put up with my mother enjoying herself while letting the household fall apart; deep down he didn't even put up with pyelonephritis and the falling apart of the entire household this entailed, because it had to go on; my father made every effort to ensure it went on. And when it had gone on, beyond the subscription concert stage, none of us would be able to set foot in the concerts any more, for my father would have already cancelled our subscriptions, that much was clear. Is that clear, my father would say, in case my mother tried to save her subscription before my father cancelled it, have I made myself clear, my father often said, or he'd say, have I not made myself clear enough, and the person being addressed would always reply in haste, oh yes, very clear. My father would also say, do we understand each other, and all of us replied in haste, yes, we do, which in fact meant that there weren't any misunderstandings in our family, nor any proscriptions; my father never proscribed anything directly, nor did he ever tell my mother not to go to the concerts. If he'd wanted her not to go to the concerts he would have quietly told her that the concerts were only for the senior employees but not the top ones, and if my mother hadn't understood that straight away, because she loved going to the concerts with their beauty, harmony and balance, qualities which were very important to my mother, he would have helped himself to a cognac and explained the difference to her again. In the end he would have said, do we understand each other, and my mother would have replied in haste that they did understand each other now. There's no need to proscribe anything in proper families, my father used to say, and it really was unnecessary because we always understood each other; and if on occasion I was stubborn and said, no way, he started from the beginning and went on until I hastily replied to his question, do we understand each other, with: yes, we do. Misunderstanding is almost impossible in a proper family, and that's why the insubordination in my question, why do the subscription concerts have to stop, couldn't be subject to any mis-understanding; it was blasphemy. And we were amazed that I wasn't struck by a sudden bolt of lightning from the heavens. Then my brother said, look, he's only human like the rest of us, and we felt a weight lift from our shoulders because we'd never dared to consider this before; no lightning bolt struck us, nor did my father appear at the door; we carried on sitting around the table like conspirators until we were seized by a bad conscience. We're so mean, my mother said sadly, we're being unfair on him. Then she sat up straight and spoke her favourite line; her favourite line was one from Fontane. There is much goodness in him, and he is as noble as a man without real love can be. Amen, my brother said, and I reminded my mother that these words were almost the last Effi utters before she dies. My mother loved *Effi Briest*, but then she pondered for a moment – fortunately catching sight of those repulsive mussels again – she pondered a while longer and said, on the other hand, hesitating slightly. Come on, say it, we told her, because we knew at once that something was coming that she'd never dared say before, and then it came out that she'd always secretly admired and worshipped Medea. We were horrified to begin with; we were the children, after all, and so would have been the ones to cop it, but my mother said, those are just fantasies, poisoning everyone and then there's peace. My mother had fanciful and exaggerated ideas, too, and now she'd just voiced them. Funnily enough, the hairs on my arms and on the rest of my body did not stand on end; after the initial shock I was very relieved, even though I would have copped it if Mum had meant it seriously, and my brother, too. No sooner had she said the Medea stuff, poisoning everyone then there's peace, than she felt absolutely awful; forgive me, dear God, she cried out, because she felt so absolutely awful, even though my mother had never believed in a dear God, not in any god, but only in harmony and human kindness, and she was dismayed at exhibiting pure wickedness rather than her normal kindness. Instead of pulling herself together as she usually did, she said that dear God would punish her dreadfully for sure; being so wicked she was bound to die this minute, but she still insisted that she admired and worshipped Medea; you're absolutely everything to me, she said, for she couldn't understand herself; nobody doubted that we were everything to our mother, nobody doubted that Medea loved her children, either; my mother couldn't understand where the kindness within her had suddenly gone; she'd really blown it with her dear God that evening, the dear God she didn't believe in. But we didn't blame our mother for wanting to poison us; we were just relieved that her accommodating, conciliatory nature, which had caused us all to suffer terribly, had disappeared for good. It was very hard for my mother to see her own ideals of harmony and human kindness fall apart; there's a big difference between silently admiring and worshipping Medea while reading *Effi Briest*, and saying it out loud; and now she had said it. Everything had fallen apart for my mother that evening because my father hadn't come home at six, as expected, and because at a quarter to ten the mussels were still in their bowl and we'd drunk *Spätlese* and hadn't switched on the news, which wasn't normal in our family; it was a quarter to ten when we looked at the clock.

All that time we hadn't looked at the clock. But when the telephone rang, the three of us looked at the clock as if by command; we felt panic and in our panic could think of nothing else, and so the first thing we did was to look at the clock, and it read a quarter to ten. Our hearts stopped, for the telephone scythed into our wickedness like God's retribution; it was the sort of telephone ring which made us think, oh, the Day of Judgement begins at a quarter to ten, we didn't know that. The ringing heralded the end of the world, at precisely the same time that everything had fallen apart for my mother, because she'd confessed that, like Medea, she'd wanted to poison us all, a thought she'd at least not had to lose much sleep over, because she never imagined she'd ever betray her fantasy, and the telephone would have to ring at that very moment, we thought. We were petrified, each of us gazed at the others' petrified faces, each one of us saw the others' bulging eyes, our faces were ashen, and once we were aware that the Day of Judgement had begun at a quarter to ten, we were aware of nothing else; we just continued staring at each other. With the telephone refusing to stop ringing I looked down at my hands and noticed

that I'd chewed my nails over the fingertips to the
raw skin; my chewed fingernails had red, bloody
edges; when I couldn't look at the red edges any
more I balled my chewed fingernails inside my fist
and gazed over at my mother. My mother hadn't
noticed the nail-chewing that evening, her fingernails
were painted a mother-of-pearl pink and looked
very pretty and groomed; she had lacquered them
that day. When my father was away on business my
mother didn't have painted nails; the paint flakes off
when you do the housework, she said, and she found
it a bore to paint her nails every other day. Besides,
my mother didn't think you needed painted nails to
look beautiful, even though my father spoke highly
of his secretary's fingernails, painted ox-blood red,
he raved about them; take a leaf out of her book, he
told my mother; it's easy for you to say, my mother
replied, when your secretary comes home in the
evening she's got all the time in the world to look
after herself, because your secretary is young, single
and childless, and so has time to groom herself and
dye her hair blonde; but then my mother did paint
her nails, she painted them mother-of-pearl pink
rather than ox-blood red, but hers were hands that
were worn from work, and if she'd chosen ox-blood
red it would have been more noticeable that my
mother's hands were worn from work. I looked at
my brother while the telephone continued ringing,

my brother noticed me looking at his hands and at once balled them into a fist so that I couldn't see the bloody edges on all ten fingers. Now I broke into a sweat; I no longer knew where to look. Amidst the ringing of the Day of Judgement my brother said hoarsely, maybe it's someone else, but no one felt the need to answer, it was just an attempt; the telephone went on ringing. And then Mum stood up. I thought, she's going to fall over; swaying, she took a few steps towards the telephone; she swayed so slowly towards the telephone that I thought, maybe she wants to give it one last chance to stop before she gets there; nobody counted but it must have rung twenty times, and none of us believed that the ringing would ever stop; for us, time after had ceased to exist, all the time in the world had shrivelled up into this ringing, none of us thought that in a quarter of an hour it would be ten o'clock, there could be no ten o'clock, time would be no more in a quarter of an hour, only this ringing, after which there'd be nothing, that much was certain. My mother walked to the living-room door with this swaying, wobbling movement, but didn't go in; she stopped at the door and held on to the frame, but the telephone didn't do her the favour of stopping. She peered into the room from the door. We couldn't see what Mum could see, or whether she'd closed her eyes; all we saw was her back in the door frame, which she held on to for a time; I'm sure the time was no longer than a second, but it was a long time, too; I felt nothing except time, which was no longer laid out before us, but had shrivelled up into this ringing of the telephone. Then my mother turned round and looked at us, not with her eyes agog as before, but calmly and thoughtfully, and then said, very clearly, on the other hand; the telephone went on ringing and my mother came back; all of a sudden she was walking fairly upright again, with just the odd sway. When she reached the table she repeated, on the other hand, louder and with determination, glaring in sheer disgust at the mussels in their bowl. She took the bowl, which had sat in front of us all evening with those vile mussels; she went into the kitchen with the mussels, and all we could hear were the shells rattling, we couldn't hear the telephone, only the shells rattling as my mother emptied the mussels into the dustbin, then she came back in and said to my brother, would you mind taking the rubbish out?

Subscribe

Subscribe to Peirene's series of books and receive three world-class contemporary European novellas throughout the year, delivered directly to your doorstep. You will also benefit from a 40% members' discount and priority booking for two people on all Peirene events.

PEIRENE'S GIFT SUBSCRIPTION
Surprise a loved one with a gift subscription. Their first book will arrive tied with a beautiful Peirene ribbon and a card with your greetings.

The perfect way for book lovers to collect all the Peirene titles.

> 'What a pleasure to receive my surprise parcel from Peirene every four months. I trust Meike to have sourced for me the most original and interesting European literature that might otherwise have escaped my attention. I love the format and look forward to having a large collection of these beautiful books. A real treat!' GERALDINE D'AMICO, DIRECTOR, JEWISH BOOK WEEK

Annual Subscription Rates
(3 books, free p&p, 40% discount on Peirene events for two people)
UK £25   EUROPE £31   REST OF WORLD £34

Peirene Press, 17 Cheverton Road, London N19 3BB
T 020 7686 1941
E subscriptions@peirenepress.com

www.peirenepress.com/shop
with secure online ordering facility

Peirene's Series

FEMALE VOICE: INNER REALITIES

NO 1
Beside the Sea by Véronique Olmi
Translated from the French by Adriana Hunter
'It should be read.' GUARDIAN

NO 2
Stone in a Landslide by Maria Barbal
Translated from the Catalan by Laura McGloughlin and Paul Mitchell
'Understated power.' FINANCIAL TIMES

NO 3
Portrait of the Mother as a Young Woman
by Friedrich Christian Delius
Translated from the German by Jamie Bulloch
'A small masterpiece.' TLS

....

MALE DILEMMA: QUESTS FOR INTIMACY

NO 4
Next World Novella by Matthias Politycki
Translated from the German by Anthea Bell
'Inventive and deeply affecting.' INDEPENDENT

NO 5
Tomorrow Pamplona by Jan van Mersbergen
Translated from the Dutch by Laura Watkinson
'An impressive work.' DAILY MAIL

NO 6
Maybe This Time by Alois Hotschnig
Translated from the Austrian German by Tess Lewis
'Weird, creepy and ambiguous.' GUARDIAN

SMALL EPIC: UNRAVELLING SECRETS

NO 7
The Brothers by Asko Sahlberg
Translated from the Finnish by Emily Jeremiah and Fleur Jeremiah
'Intensely visual.' INDEPENDENT ON SUNDAY

NO 8
The Murder of Halland by Pia Juul
Translated from the Danish by Martin Aitken
'A brilliantly drawn character.' TLS

NO 9
Sea of Ink by Richard Weihe
Translated from the Swiss German by Jamie Bulloch
'Delicate and moving.' INDEPENDENT

....
NEW IN 2013
TURNING POINT:
REVOLUTIONARY MOMENTS

NO 10
The Mussel Feast by Birgit Vanderbeke
Translated from the German by Jamie Bulloch
'An extraordinary book.' STANDPOINT

NO 11
Mr Darwin's Gardener by Kristina Carlson
Translated from the Finnish by Emily Jeremiah and Fleur Jeremiah
'Effortless humour.' SUOMEN KUVALEHTI

NO 12
Chasing the King of Hearts by Hanna Krall
Translated from the Polish by Philip Boehm
'An outstanding writer.' GAZETA WYBORCZA

Peirene

Contemporary European Literature. Thought provoking, well designed, short.

'Two-hour books to be devoured in a single sitting: literary cinema for those fatigued by film.' TLS